ALEXANDRA CAMPBELL:

Private Eye

A NOVEL BY

MORRIGAN DEWME

- ALEXANDRA CAMPBELL: PRIVATE EYE Copyright ©2021
- Line By Lion Publications
- www.pixelandpen.studio
- ISBN: 978-1-948807-99-9
-
-
-
- Cover Art:Thomas Lamkin Jr.
- Editing By:Ian Jedlica
-

LINE BY LION
PUBLICATIONS

Chapter One

PRIVATE investigator Alexandra Campbell opened her eyes. With one arm, she pushed her mane of tawny hair out of her face. The other arm, unfortunately, remained pinned under the portly accountant who still slept. She was further pinned by one doughy pale arm, and he was exhaling gusts of last night's wine, a magnificently terrible Merlot, into her face with every breath. He snored. Loudly.

Alex lay there, contemplating the six tiny coarse hairs that grew out of the bridge of his nose as she debated her next move. This investigation had been a long one (pun absolutely intended as well as not applicable), and the gentleman in question had been speaking rhapsodically about love and marriage and, at least, a "romantic day in." None of which were a part of Alex's plan. She had an appointment early that afternoon, with the portly accountant's employer to be exact. Thus, stealth was of the utmost importance, unless she wanted things to get messy. Alex loathed messy; she avoided it at every possible point.

Excruciatingly slowly, Alex eased her arm out from under the man she had been interrogating for six weeks. Her hand was asleep, cold and clammy, and she shook it gently, keeping one wary eye on his face. He didn't move. Once the feeling had returned to her arm, Alex moved to phase two of her plan. She eased her free leg and arm off the edge of the bed, lowering them and letting gravity take her with deliberate nonchalance, to the ground. The last 18 inches went more quickly than she'd anticipated, and with a thud far louder than the acrobat's landing she had planned, Alex was free. He stopped snoring with a snort. His name was Fred Langley, which added another layer of difficulty to the case as it was incredibly difficult to yell "Fred" with sincere passion and ecstasy. Alex froze, her brown eyes wide. After a second, he rolled over and the rhythmic sounds started again. Alex heaved a sigh of relief and began army crawling to the foot of the bed.

She found her panties, black lace of course, and slid them on before peeking, Kilroy-like up to the bed. Fred was still sleeping. God bless Fred. And Merlot. And multiple orgasms. She stood and looked for her bra. It was nowhere to be found. Damn it. She'd liked that one. Oh well, it couldn't be helped. She slid her dress, thanking the deities of fashion for sheaths, over her head. She twisted to reach the zipper and nearly fell, banging her hip on the dresser with a muffled curse. Fine, she'd fix it in the elevator. Alex grabbed her clutch and strappy sandals and left the room, dangling the shoes from her fingers and closing the door in slow motion. Once it had latched she sprinted for the elevator, pushing the button five times in a row.

"Come on," she whispered. "Comeoncomeoncomeon." It took an eternity, and by the time it arrived, Alex vibrated with impatience, convinced that the device had stopped on every floor, and had nearly given herself whiplash checking the hallway behind her. The doors opened with a bing. "Shhhh,"

Alex reprimanded, before shaking her head at herself in chagrin. "Sorry," she apologized to the machine and shook her head again.

By the time she arrived in the lobby, Alex had arranged herself and her shoes clicked in sophisticated rhythm across the tiles. Her phone beeped, telling her that her ride was waiting.

"Checking out?" the lobby clerk asked with a smile and a raised eyebrow. Charles was one of Alex's favorite people, and with this particular hotel being a popular venue, she had spoken with him often. He was one of very few people who knew what she truly did for a living, and had always treated her with dignity and professionalism, if not a little wry humor. Such candor was rare, and in response she tipped well.

"Something like that," she replied.

"Very good Ms. Campbell, we will look forward to seeing you again." Alex flipped a wave over her shoulder and headed for the door. She checked her phone. If she hurried, she would have time to go home and take a shower before her appointment. That was good. She desperately wanted a shower.

The driver had been watching porn and masturbating. There was no sign of it in the car, no smell, and he was nothing but courteous and polite, but she could tell. Alex could always tell, it was what her Grandmother had called her "gift" above Alex's extreme protestations. Her Grandma had had a bit of it herself, as Alex had discovered when the old woman had caught her making herself throw up after a meal in a desperate attempt at some sort of control. Puberty had brought with it, in addition to the normal whirlwind of hormones and the sudden betrayal of her parents' divorce, a sudden window into the rest of the world. Suddenly, Alex could see everyone's deepest and darkest secrets and the revelation effectively shattered the shreds of innocence that she had managed to maintain. Infidelity, lies, pettiness, thefts, they were all there in front of her in technicolor. Thus, when her grandmother caught her she confessed to everything in shuddering sobs that were part shame and part relief. Her Grandmother's' gift was activated and revealed itself by smell; certain smells would mean one things or another, happiness, sadness, lies.

"So that's how you knew I was feeding Millie my vegetables," Alex exclaimed, referring to her Grandmother's ancient, cataract-blinded poodle.

"And that it was you who had broken my vase," her Grandmother replied. For Alex, it was sight, and as the storms of puberty passed she realized that they centered around arousal. Almost any time she focused, Alex could pick up on strong emotion, maybe get a vision behind it. If she were aroused, or the person around her was very aroused, she could see colors, auras almost, and flashes of insight. An orgasm was, quite literally, an eye into someone's soul. Losing her virginity had been a tragedy on many levels thanks to her insight, and Alex had been terrified that she'd never have a "normal" sex life. But her Grandmother, poking at her computer through dial-up, had discovered that onyx was sometimes thought to block psychic abilities, and bought her a beautiful cabochon that she still had, and treasured.

"Red Jasper increases libido," her grandmother had told her, pronouncing it li-by-dough, "but I'll let you get your own of those." She had managed to hone her skills, turn them into an extremely lucrative career, but at times like this, as she ignored the magenta aura swirling inside the car, bringing with it the driver's hopes for that night, it was nothing but a nuisance.

*   *   *

ALEX'S cell phone beeped. She looked at it with a mixture of hope and mild consternation, assuming that either Fred had woken up and noticed her absence, or her husband Neil's flight had arrived early. Instead, the handsome face of Hank Barnett, detective at the 22nd Precinct, looked up at her. Hank was a rare find, someone who knew about her unique skills but had continued to treat her with respect. She had been nervous when he was first hired, replacing the affable dinosaur Detective Hannah, with whom she had a longstanding professional understanding. Imagine her surprise when Hank had become more than just a client, but a friend.

She thumbed the green button and held the phone to her ear. "Good morning, Detective," she chirped.

"Morning?" he teased, "some of us have been up since five, you slacker."

"Perks of self-employment," Alex replied. "My boss is a bitch, but I can sleep in if I want to. What's up?" Hank sighed. She could imagine him running his fingers through his thick hair, making it stand up in clumps and spikes.

"We could really use your help," he said. "When can you come in?"

Alex chewed her full lower lip and contemplated. She had an appointment with Fred's boss around noon, and then this evening Neil would be home, which means she had several hours of "of course I clean while you are gone" cleaning to catch up on.

"Late this afternoon," she said at last, "will that work?"

"Absolutely," Hank replied. "Looking forward to it."

He hung up, and Alex looked out the window with a small smirk on her face. One case solved, guarantee of more money (albeit lesser amounts of government-controlled money) coming in, her husband coming home, and an afternoon spent in the company of one of her best friends. It was shaping up to be a wonderful day.

Chapter Two

ALEX had time for an effective if unsatisfactory shower, holding her head carefully away from the spray to avoid the hassle of either a blow dryer or dripping ends. She went to her closet and picked out one of her most basic and severe outfits, black blazer, black skirt, and white blouse, what her friend Pasha called her "Power Bitch" suit. She kept her makeup light and neutral, and clasped a long silver chain around her neck. Her heels clacking, she headed out the door with fifteen minutes to spare. *Norton's Management Incorporated* was in one of the few skyscrapers that lined the Ohio River, a building not unlike the one her husband worked in, on the few occasions that he was in town. Alex sat in the conference room, gazing at the green, sluggish water and the barges that putted up and down, sinking low in the water with their cargo. Her report was on the table in front of her in a discreet manila envelope. Richard Lowe, the man who had hired her for this job, among others, entered. He was followed by a towering Frankenstein of a man, his thinning hair brushed back over a spot more bald than thin. He had beady eyes under bulging and bushy brows and a knowing smile.

"So," he boomed, "this is our little detective." Alex felt the muscles in her jaw tighten, but forced her mouth into a smile. "Indeed," she said, extending her hand and grasping his. She could feel his eyes crawling over her like bugs. She sighed inwardly. Inevitably, it came to this; the man who saw her only for the sex and not her expertise. She would make this report as brief of possible.

Turning away from the Neanderthal, she handed the file to Richard. His smile seemed apologetic. "Everything is here," she said, "bank accounts, the affected clients, approximate dates and amounts."

"Thank y—" Richard began. His courtesy was cut off by an indulgent chuckle.

"Forgive me for asking," the Neanderthal said, in a way that made it clear that he was not, in the least, apologetic, "but how can we possibly tell if this information is reliable?"

"Ms. Campbell has completed satisfactory inves—" continued Richard.

"Well, even a broken clock is right twice a day," the Neanderthal said with a simian grin. He turned to Alex, who could feel her blood pumping in her temples. "What guarantee can you give that your... unconventional approach actually works?"

Alex had a canned speech that she used in these situations. It included a list of times she had been called as an expert witness, her curriculum vitae, and her education. Today, however, she decided to take a more direct approach. She sauntered over to the towering man and stared through her lashes into his eyes. Her pink tongue darted out, briefly, moistening her lips. She slid one hand up his torso from his waist to his shoulder, grabbing him when he moved away in surprise. With the other hand, she reached below his belt. His eyes widened in surprise. However, she quickly located evidence that he was not entirely displeased by the attention. Alex closed her eyes and focused. The information came slowly, she had not prepared herself, mentally, physically, or otherwise, for an investigation, but her brow furrowed and eventually it came.

"You were supposed to have a date last night," she murmured. "Someone you met online. You bought flowers and sat at the table for two hours. She never came. You went home and watched porn."

His eyes, which had grown steadily larger since the moment Alex approached him, were bulging by the time he pulled indignantly away. He was panting slightly. The large man cleared his throat, straightened his tie, and looked at Mr. Lowe.

"Tell Mr. Langley to meet me in my office," he said, and strode out of the room.

"I apologize for any discomfort," Alex said to Richard.

He chuckled. "You have nothing to apologize for. We are very grateful for your help." He shook Alex's hand, and handed her a check. There were three zeroes after the first number.

"If you ever need my help again, just ask," Alex replied.

*   *   *

Alex thought about going home for a bit, but instead she headed down to the station. She pulled into the parking lot, reaching into her glove compartment for the parking pass and her onyx necklace. The necklace was heavy, a large black cabochon suspended from a silver chain. The gift from her grandmother was tarnished and worn, but it still helped to dull Alex's gift. She was never sure if it was a placebo effect or the actual properties of the stone, and frankly she didn't care. She had donned it religiously for over two decades whenever she needed a break from her power. She had learned, after her first disastrous visit, never to go into the station without something to help dull the roar. She clasped the necklace under her hair, the stone's cool weight resting just above her breasts. She strode through the front door of the police station, flashing her ID at Randy. The officer was a familiar face who smiled and pressed the button to allow her in the doors while maintaining a stone face of neutrality at the woman who insisted that her right to privacy superseded his right to check her bag and informed him that if he did not let her enter unsearched he would be hearing from her lawyer. Alex nodded, somewhat more coolly, at the rail-thin Sergeant Lawrence, currently manning the front desk. When Alex had first begun conducting investigations for the department, Sergeant Lawrence had somehow heard the details of her expertise and responded by making a series of inappropriate and degrading remarks, loudly and to no one in particular, every time she visited. One day, she had taken him aside and explained in no uncertain terms that the Sergeant could either cease and desist with the comments or she would be more than happy to tell his fellow officers exactly what kinds of clubs he liked to visit on his days off and which animal his custom suit portrayed. They had both enjoyed an uneasy truce since then. Well, Alex enjoyed it anyway. Sergeant Lawrence remained wary.

One lobby and three hallways later and Alex found herself, as always, increasingly grateful for her necklace. She had been skeptical at first, not believing that a stone could have any sort of effect of dampening her visions, when so much had not. The station was full, and each room held a bubble of rage or pain or confusion, which, left unguarded, pounded their way into her head, even when she could not see the source or the details. The necklace kept it all to a dull roar. Still she was happy to shut the door behind her and enter the sanctuary of Detective Henry Barnett's office. Detective Barnett, or Hank, as he had been since six months into their working relationship, was a marked improvement on his predecessor. While both men treated her with credulity and respect, Hank's warmth and humor had rapidly moved him from client to friend. He seemed genuinely happy to see her, beaming from the window with his hand pressing his cell phone to his ear. With the other hand, he gestured to a chair, a sweet smile crossing his handsome face. He had gotten thinner since the last time Alex had seen him; his pants hung loosely from his narrow waist and thin lines, not caused by laughter, ran outwards from the corner of his azure eyes. He ended the call curtly, running his hand through his caramel hair, as always just a little too long to be strictly regulation. Even so, he put one arm around her in a brief hug before settling with a sigh on his desk. Alex, perceiving his hurry, decided to relieve him of the necessity of small talk and preliminaries.

"How can I help, Hank?" She knew that she did not imagine the look of relief that crossed his face.

"Do you remember the college professor who was murdered two months ago?"

Alex nodded. The murder had been all over the news. Opinion columns had been filled to the brim with one side decrying guns and the other deriding the students and the need for "grieving spaces." Alex quite hastily grew disgusted and overwhelmed with it all and tuned out. Nothing, it seemed, was sacred anymore when people recruited the dead to use as bludgeons to further their cause.

"You need my help with him," she asked. Hank grimaced.

"Yes and no. Three weeks ago I got a call from our ballistics guys. Turns out the same gun that killed him had also been involved in the murder of," he flipped over a manila folder, "24 -year- old Kisha Dowe. When I heard that I had them check other cases with the same caliber bullet. The killer used a 40 caliber, which is rare. There were five bullets that matched the rifling patterns."

"So, it's a serial killer," Alex asked incredulously. Hank attempted a grin in a charming but ineffectual stab at his usual good humor.

"You've been watching too many cop shows again," he said. Alex blushed.

"Guilty, Detective. Besides, if I call it research then I can write off *Netflix* as a business expense." Hank shook his head and grinned.

"All that we know for now is that the same weapon was used. I've been over the files a million times and I can't find a single thing that links the victims. Nothing. I was hoping you could help with that."

Alex flipped through the files, cringing at the gruesome post-mortem photographs.

"Hank, these murders took place weeks, sometimes months ago; what did you want me to do?"

He fidgeted a bit with his keys, the muscles in his jaw jumping. "I thought that maybe there might be… vibes or something you could pick up on."

"Now who's been watching too much TV?" Alex asked.

Hank's shoulders deflated. "Well, maybe you could go with me to talk to the families," he countered, "something?"

Alex sighed. "I'll try, Hank, for you. But you know it doesn't really work like that and I'm not promising anything, do you hear me?"

Hank nodded, his mouth set in a grim line. Alex stood, giving his arm an affectionate squeeze.

"Call me if anything else comes up, the sooner the better. Can I take this?" she asked, holding up the folder.

Hank opened his mouth to speak, but then his phone rang and so he simply nodded and Alex let herself out of the office, shutting the door gently behind her. There, trapped in the narrow hallway, Alex clutched her onyx tightly and took a deep breath. More people had come into the station while she had been buffered by Hank and the thick oak door, and for reasons she didn't like to think about being with him made her a bit more receptive. She walked quickly across the linoleum floor, glancing at the time on the face of her cell phone. She was running late. A photograph of her with her husband Neil smiled back from behind the digital number. Big Pine Key. That picture was ten years old. Neil had wanted to go all the way to Key West, two or three islands down, but she'd insisted that they stay at the little B&B instead of a hotel. She'd given lots of reasons, less crowded, less expensive, the joy of seeing the tiny, knee-high key deer, these were all valid. Still, more than anything, Alex had known that were she to spend her entire vacation within the psychic reach of Duvall Street or one of the main resorts catering to the newlywed, she'd come home utterly depleted. They'd had a wonderful time. Alex caught herself smiling down at the phone. Maybe tonight she'd ask him about planning another vacation. It had been too long.

Alex pushed through the door back to the lobby and all thoughts of vacations and smiles disappeared. Pain. So much pain. Alex scanned the crowd until she saw her. The girl had the socially malnourished look of the unpopular teen and her feet, clad in a pair of heavily tattooed Chucks, tapped the floor in a staccato rhythm. She chewed on one end of her hair. Alex sopped, involuntarily, ten feet away. The pain, the need, was like walking into a brick wall. Alex had learned years ago that to ignore these impulses could have catastrophic results, a tragic night at a subway station came to mind, and so she stood still, waiting. Slowly the girl's eyes, hazed and haunted, rose to meet her own. With that, Alex could SEE. She saw notes left in a locker and the hopes and dreams they inspired. She saw late night chats on Facebook or on the phone. She saw the girl experimenting with makeup and outfits, carefully curated from fashion magazines, and she saw a desperate, all-encompassing desire to be one of the popular girls. Then, she saw the high heels thrown across the floor as she was held on the bed, heard the girl's screams. Alex shook her head once to clear it. She'd seen enough. She moved towards the girl, slowly, hands up, approaching her like she would a wounded animal, and crouched on her knees by the scrawled upon shoes. Katey. Her name was Katey. Alex's voice was low and soft, few people who knew Alex would have recognized it.

"Katey," she said. "I'm Alex. May I touch your hands?"

The girl's eyes widened a bit and she nodded.

"Katey, I know what happened. It was not your fault. Being popular does not excuse his behavior. And you are NOT alone."

Giant tears welled up in Katey's eyes. In her mother's as well as the woman drew her daughter closer. "How do you know all of this?" It was little more than a whisper.

"It's my job," Alex replied. "I'm going to give you a card now…" Gingerly, she reached into her purse and pulled out one of Hank's business cards. "Take this to the desk and ask to see this man. Tell him I gave this to you. He'll take good care of you."

"Promise?" Alex felt a flicker of hope from the girl.

"I promise." Alex stood and brushed the dirt off her stockings and walked out the door. Hank did not need another case right now, but she knew he wouldn't mind. He was a sucker for a damsel in distress, which explained why he had never given her so much as a second glance. Sure, they had lunch together, talked on the phone sometimes, but friendship was as far as it went. Most of the time, Alex was grateful. Ever since her breasts had come in just shy of her 14th birthday Alex had always chafed under the attention of admirers. It was nice to find a gentleman. Still, sometimes it made her wonder if she was losing her touch.

Speaking of touch, she had to hurry if she was going to be able to prepare for her evening. Neil was due home in a matter of hours, and she had big plans. A month was a very long time to go without, and work sex didn't count. She slid into the car, the seat cool against her thighs, and drove home. Moments later, after a brief stop at the grocery store, she was gliding into the sleek subdivision on the east end of town. She reached the end of her cul-de-sac and pulled into the driveway of an immaculately kept if nondescript Cape Cod residence and eased into her garage. Hopping out of the car and glancing at the clock, she keyed her code into the discreet keypad and let herself in. Her heels clicked rapidly as she crossed to the kitchen and set the bags on the gray granite countertop. She regretted making the decision to stop by the police department, as it cut drastically into her preparation time; she had a little, but not a lot. To quote her friend Selah, "the dead aren't going anywhere fast." Selah Agape, born Sarah Rosenblum, was Alex's oldest friend in the city, and the first person who, hearing about Alex's gift, hadn't made her feel like a freak or worse. Alex made a mental note to call her, and snipped three blue hydrangea heads from her bushes outside the front door. She arranged them simply in a large glass bowl and nodded. It was nice to be home; she'd spent a lot of time away lately. She walked through the quiet rooms, stepping around the sparse designer furniture, her feet swishing against the deep piled carpet. Her home was her sanctuary, hers and Neil's, and everything in it was cool neutrals. Gray walls, cream trim. She straightened one of the throw pillows that lay, knocked sideways. Alex crossed to the kitchen and poured herself a glass of wine. She reached under the cabinet and pulled out her slow cooker, a wedding gift from one of Neil's relatives. She had registered for a dozen or more kitchen gadgets in the year between their engagement and their wedding, full of dreams of elegant gourmet meals. It hadn't been long, however, before Alex realized that she was a terrible cook and had neither the patience nor desire to improve. As such, one by one, the devices had been sold or donated. The slow cooker had remained; it was great for heating up soup. She opened two containers of such now, a heady, spiced minestrone from the local deli, and poured them into the cooker's glass container, setting it to low. She took a sip of wine, feeling her shoulders relax, and mixed together a simple salad, topping it with strawberries, sliced almonds and blue cheese crumbles and dressing it with a simple vinaigrette. She lit a few candles, nodded again, and carried her wine to the bathroom.

She turned the water on, set the warmth, at just a notch below "flesh-searing," and set her phone in its base. She reached out with one manicured hand and touched a couple of screens on her phone. "Sister Christian" filled the room. Alex exhaled, feeling some of the tension leave her shoulders, and poured a generous dollop of coconut scented bath salts into the tub. If '80s music and the smell of the beach didn't help her ready herself for her husband's return, nothing would. Her clothes crumpled to the floor with a low "whoosh," and she stepped into the tub. Warm, scented steam enveloped her as she settled into the water, and "Sister Christian" and its motorin' gave way to Tone Loc busting a move and then to Mr. Big. Years of unofficial research had led Alex to believe that men were primarily concerned with the cleanliness of a woman's breasts. At least, when showering with a man her breasts received special and extensive attention. When Alex wanted to prepare herself, however, she focused on other areas, running her hands in slow circles behind her knees, languorous strokes up the insides of her thighs or along the delicate planes of her neck. Her painted toes turned the faucet on again and again, refilling the hot water. She didn't have to bother with shaving, at least, Pasha, her brilliant Romanian accountant, had showed her how to make trips to the salon, the gym, and the dermatologist business expenses, bless him, and so her time was true luxury. She checked the time again. Neil wouldn't be home for a couple of hours. She slid her hand below the water. Self-care, as Selah often reminded her, was very important.

Chapter Three

COIFFED, made-up, and primed rather than sated, Alex curled herself into a winged back chair with a book and a cool, crisp glass of Moscato. Her wine snob friends mocked her for this preference, but she didn't care. Let them have their tannins and their 'earthy notes' and their 'must get accustomed to it' palates. The world was hard enough, Alex didn't want to drink something she had to work to enjoy. The book was fluff as well, brain candy. Sweet with little nutritional value. Her husband, Neil, made a great show of reading Dostoyevsky, Descartes. He read them so thoroughly that he'd been working on a collection of each for years, now read mostly when she pulled out her latest paperback or guests attended their once-frequent dinner parties. Alex had read them all as well, either in college or as an attempt to bond with Neil, but they weren't what she enjoyed. The spine cracked satisfyingly when Alex opened the book, effectively numbing it, or so she hoped, from the inevitable dogeared pages or drops in the tub. Ten minutes. She suppressed a silly grin imagining Neil walking through the door, even more handsome than the day they met, his jacket over his shoulder and a smile of approval as he smelled the soup and saw the scotch she'd left on the counter. An hour later, she stood to fill her glass, again, and turn the crock pot from low to warm. She checked her phone, but there were no new messages since the last time she'd looked about a minute before. Her stomach grumbled, and she opened her book again with a sigh. Seconds later, she closed it. It was pointless; she had read the same chapter a dozen times.

Looking around, she saw some dust had collected on the crystal and chrome picture frames that graced the mantle. She wiped them down, smiling and stroking them with her finger. Though not the most attractive of photos, still they meant so much. Her grandmother, a psychic of no little talent herself, had guided Alex through a particularly painful and enlightening puberty. A string of four pictures of her and Neil in a little photo booth, a ridiculous sentimental souvenir from their first date. Their first Christmas, posed with Tiki, the cat that was the closest thing to a child that they would ever have. Neil's parents, stolid and upright even in a picture. This task tended to, Alex threw away the paper towel she had used to clean, then rushed across the room when her phone vibrated. It was Pasha, with some witty oeuvre that Alex couldn't bring herself to respond to. She started to text Neil, then backspaced furiously. He had told her repeatedly that he hated getting texts when he was travelling; they only made him take more time to get home if he had to stop to respond. She tossed her phone on the table with more force than she intended, and it slid onto the floor. She left it there and turned on the television. After 15 minutes she realized that she couldn't remember what show she was watching. Finally, at 9:00 she gave in and ate. The dinner, at least, was everything she hoped, though the company was not, and she ate curled up in the same wingback chair, staring distractedly out the window.

The rest of the night shattered into agonizingly small chunks of time. Loading the dishwasher – 6 minutes. Checking her email – 3 minutes. Updating her calendar – 4 minutes. Her greatest achievement was finally beating a level of Cookie Crusher on her phone that had had her stumped for a week. Eventually she washed off her makeup and changed into her pajamas. She considered putting on something slinky, but then threw it into the hamper and pulled on some fleece pants and a Bush concert t-shirt that was older than her marriage. She scrolled through favorite videos on her television and brought up bedtime yoga. The wine had worn off hours before, leaving the bitter aftertaste of disappointment and anger. Alex knew that to sleep in that state was an invitation for nightmares. Balahanda – why does he always do this. Salabhana – don't' fight to breathe. It wasn't his fault, he got held up. Again. Sarasana – the least he could do was text. She looked pretty hot, too. She held the corpse pose for a solid 20 minutes, breathing out her frustration until at last she felt calm. "Namaste," she said to the ceiling fan, and climbed into bed.

*   *   *

A fluff of cool air and a shift of the mattress roused Alex as Neil climbed into bed beside her. He settled, curled slightly into an apostrophe, his knees pointing away. Alex rolled sleepily toward him, sliding her hand under his shirt and across the curve of his stomach. The muscles jumped at her touch. She stretched around, not without some difficulty at that angle, and planted a kiss on the back of his neck.

"Hey babe," she murmured, "welcome home."

"Good to be here," he said and reached back to pat her thigh.

Alex snuggled closer, breathing in his scent and sliding her hand under the waistband of his pants. He stopped breathing and she felt his body go rigid, though not the part that she had hoped. His hand left her thigh to stop hers.

"Not tonight okay baby," he said. "I'm really tired."

"Okay," Alex said, swallowing past the knot that suddenly formed in her throat. As Pasha had once said, you never got secure or mature enough that rejection from a loved one didn't sting. Considering his age and experience, Alex figured he would know.

"Glad you're home."

*　　　*　　　*

Alex woke to light filtering through the gauzy curtains and buzzing coming from her cell phone. "Mmph," she grumbled and slapped the face of the device until she'd managed to turn the alarm off. She stretched, feeling her muscles pop as she pushed her hands over her head, arching her back. She touched Neil lightly on the shoulder.

"Are you going in today?" she asked.

Sometimes after a long trip, he took the day off. Neil inhaled, rubbing his hand rapidly over the stubble that sprouted, surprisingly dark as always, on his chin.

"Yeah," he said. Alex pursed her lips and summoned her courage.

"Can you be a little late? Coffee plus?" He smiled, the charming boyish smile she'd fallen in love with years before.

"I think I can do that," he said. Alex beamed and brushed his hair back from his forehead.

"I'll start the coffee," she said.

"Hurry."

His laughter followed her as she walked down the hall, an extra bounce in her step. She didn't need him, the relationship had never been built on need and on some level, she knew that he couldn't bear it if it had, but want? She wanted him. His laugh, his calm sturdiness. His body. Just the warmth of having him near her. She'd admit to want. On her way back to the bedroom she stopped at the bathroom door. Her onyx necklace lay on the counter where she'd taken it off the night before. Usually she wore it when they were together; to not do so felt like spying. Sometimes it even felt like work and she didn't want that. Still something, some tinge, told her to forego it and so she shrugged and moved on. She'd learned long before to trust her intuition when it came, to listening to the "whispers" as her Grandmother had called them. Her neck bare, Alex continued down the hall.

She paused in the doorway and pulled her shirt slowly over her head, feeling the fabric catch for a brief second on her nipples, and well aware of the picture she made in the silvery morning light. She saw the bulk of him, even through the heavy down comforter, and knew she'd had the effect that she'd wanted. She slid her pants down over the swell of her hips and to the floor, careful as she stepped out of them. Years in her profession and an ever-growing awareness of her body had given her a grace more than most, and yet there was the small part of her brain that was always afraid that she would trip. She did not, she rarely did, and she padded across the rug to the bed, keeping her eyes on Neil's. He threw the blanket back as she arrived, and she saw that he had not wasted time while she'd been gone. Joyful laughter bubbled up in her throat at the sight of him, supine and naked, and she straddled him, leaning back so that the top of his sexual organ brushed against hers lightly. She kissed him, gently at first and then deep. He groaned and shifted his hips while his hands played with the delicate and sensitive skin at the small of her back. She teased him for a moment, feeling her body and her mind open, feeling him grow even harder until with a moan he put his hands on her breasts. She allowed him to drive, to pull her down on him, lifting her hips up and down slowly. Her mouth opened in an "O" of pleasure as her eyes closed and he slid deeply in. She rocked her hips in a circle, feeling the electric, not-quite painful, jolt as he rubbed against her G spot, her breath coming faster and he drove deeper still. The visions began to flow through his mind to hers, first a trickle, then a flood and she dove into them, wanting to see herself as he saw her. She screamed out, at first nearing pleasure as she felt his need, saw her breasts bounce and the curve of her neck. Except... Alex's eyes flew open in shock and she forced them shut before Neil could tell that something was wrong. She kept her hips moving with an effort born of willpower to an extent she didn't know she had.

The neck, the breasts she had seen were not hers. There was a mole that she didn't have, the skin was silkily dark. The cascade of hair that swung behind the woman's shoulders was a chocolatey brunette. Alex moaned, a sound she hoped sounded longing, and forced herself to look deeper. Faster. The tremble in his legs and frantic pumping of his hips let her know she didn't have much time. She looked and saw, to her horror, the lobby of a hotel. Swanky, all chrome and marble. She heard a woman's throaty laugh, saw Neil walking into a hotel room, and felt his lust as a hand took his. "Well we could kill her," the woman's voice said, playfully, in the dark. She saw that thought grow, become real. Her heartbeat quickened, and she grew nauseous but still she squeezed his member with her vagina, drawing out his passion, drawing her deeper. She saw money exchanging hands, smelled cigarette smoke. "I'll text you where she'll be." Saw cold, dead snake eyes. Neil yelled with release and she was in terror, the scenes fading away as he spilled into her. Alex toppled off him, turning away, not willing to see more.

They lay, panting for various reasons, next to each other. Neil smiled at her and she managed, somehow, to smile back. "Don't let him know," she told herself. She made herself keep smiling, and hoped it didn't look like the rictus it felt to her.

"Thank you," Neil said, kissing her neck. She ran her fingers through his hair, a habit that, until that morning, had brought her inexpressible comfort and joy.

"No, thank you," she insisted, determined to keep the tears at bay until he went to the shower. Then she turned her face into the pillow and wept.

Chapter Four

NEIL took long showers. Extremely long showers. Sometimes this irritated Alex to no end, especially if there was something she needed out of his bathroom or some tidbit of information that she needed to have. This time, though, she was grateful. While he lathered, rinsed, repeated and whatever, she took the time to cry again, releasing her hurt, betrayal and rage. The top layers of it, anyway. The rest were going to take time and with time at a premium, she felt her steel taking over. That calm, cool force that crammed whatever emotions weren't helpful into a box, slammed and locked the door, and left them behind to deal with at a more convenient time. Some of the boxes behind that watertight door had been there for years gathering dust and waiting for a time that never seemed to come. Others had, at least in her imagination, caution tape wrapped around them and contained memories and feeling that were, and were likely to remain too big, too much. Her therapist regularly encouraged her to explore those boxes and she would, someday. Today, though, she would get out of bed. She would wash her face again and sleek her hair back into a ponytail. She rubbed some concealer around her eyes and dabbed on a little bit of foundation. Foundation generally meant mascara, or she ran the risk of her fair lashes disappearing altogether, but she decided to forego it. She had the sneaking suspicion that she would be scrubbing it from her cheeks once she was in the sanctity of Selah's salon. She poured coffee, filling her silver insulated travel mug all the way to the top and rushing out the door before Neil managed to deplete their hot water tank. She realized after she'd pulled out of the driveway that she had no idea where she planned to go.

She drove, picking rights and lefts seemingly at random until she found herself at Taylor Park. Filled with ancient trees and peacefully burbling fountains, it was one of her favorite green sanctuaries in the chaos of the city. Even the statues looked serene, thoughtful in their eternal gaze. Admittedly, people had frequented it less since the body of a beloved college professor had been found, with two seemingly impersonal bullets in the back of his head. Alex climbed out of the car, feeding the meter from the cache of change that she kept in her console for just that reason. She slid her earbuds in and scrolled through her playlist, looking for anything that might prime her pump. Her red jasper tinkled at her wrist. She had swallowed her vitamins, a combination of B Complex, guarana and more that she had found heightened her senses, on the way there. She rejected one song after another. They all just irritated her somehow. "That 'I love you' that they sing of? 'The One' that's going to last forever, it won't. It will die. And someday, possibly, for no reason other than the whim of someone else, so will you." Alex sighed heavily. Today was, perhaps, not the best day to begin this investigation. Still it beat mooning around the house, trying to avoid Neil until he left for work. She was not there at any rate. She would just have to fake it until she made it. It wouldn't be the first time. She thought wryly, her mind wandering to those awful teenaged sexcapades. "He rubs my clit like it's a magic lamp," she'd complained to her best friend while they pretended to smoke, and practice being jaded. "I wonder what he thinks is going to pop out." "I think he's more concerned about what's popping in," her friend had countered, and they'd laughed, spraying themselves with fruit-scented perfume before heading back to school. Finally, she decided on a playlist called "Girl Power" — Alanis, Gwen, Adele, that's exactly what she needed. She walked, slowly, through the park, making her way along the winding paths to the makeshift shrine that had been erected. Framed pictures, flowers, bottles of scotch were arranged haphazardly but neatly as well as more personal items such as carved animal totems and political buttons. Alex ran her hands over them. There was emotion here, all right. Lots of it, and not all of it the bittersweet combination of love and melancholy that she expected. Something else jarred, one note off in a chord, every now and then. Alex's brow furrowed. She couldn't put her finger on what she sensed, it was too old, too amorphous, but she made a note of it to follow up on later. In her ears, Adele was singing from the other side. Alex snickered despite herself. Irony was funny no matter the situation. She checked the time. 10:30. Good. Selah would be in her salon.

Alex's route took her close to the University; she left the freeway with the billboards screaming about "a cleaner, more efficient future" that had sprung up like weeds the past few months, and began to navigate the narrow, bricked streets. She drove past the noodle shops, the poster and record havens, the trendy shoppes with "unique imported gifts" that could be found at every shop just like it all over the country, and finally to the rows of old houses turned apartments. Selah's place was amongst those, stately almost-Victorian. Alex eschewed the parking lot, it only had 4 spaces and often grew crowded after lunch, and parked on the street. She entered, pushing through the beaded curtain and gonging the bells, breathing in the smell of herbs and incense that, as their friendship had deepened, had come to mean safety.

"Honey, I'm home," she called.

A clatter of beads and Selah appeared, tall and majestic as ever clutching a mug of tea in one hand.

"Darling," she said, and they embraced. Alex found herself blinking back tears once again. They parted, and Selah's brows came together.

"You look absolutely awful."

Alex laughed and then the tears began to flow in earnest. She had met Selah at a yoga class, had spent three classes feeling a strange, almost tidal pull, a release of tension that she attributed to the breathing and the motions before she finally looked around and saw Salah's eyes and open smile.

"You too?" The woman had asked that day in the locker room. Alex had been confused and so Selah had leaned in.

"Your gift," she said. Or curse; I can't tell which yet. Alex had smiled then, and taken a breath deeper than any she had taken since her grandmother had died.

"I can't either," she replied.

"Why don't you come to one of our lunches."

"Our?" Alex had asked.

"We are a sort of unofficial club," Selah had answered. "People who are special. Like you."

She handed Alex her business card.

"Thursdays around noon. Maybe we can figure it out together."

Their friendship had deepened quickly from that point on. Selah was not, strictly speaking, psychic. She did however have a gift. She could look at a person and know, instinctively and instantly, exactly what they needed to hear at that moment. Not wanted, Selah would say ruefully on many occasions, but needed. It made her, ironically, and incredibly effective and popular, if not an incredibly accurate, fortune teller.

"Why this?" Alex had asked once, over steaming bowls of Pho. Selah had smiled then, a serene smile.

"Why not?" she asked.

"Well," Alex replied, "you could have done anything. You could have done something real. A political advisor or a congressperson. Get involved in laws or foreign affairs."

"Tell me," Selah wasn't mad, not necessarily, but there was an edge to her voice. "How many degrees, how many years would it take for a black woman in Kentucky to gain office? The kind of office you need to have that level of effect? And even if I did, how much more would I have to do to be taken seriously?"

Alex opened her mouth, closed it. Opened it again. Closed it again.

"Exactly." Selah had said. She leaned forward, warming her hands on the side of her bowl. "This," she motioned at the beads and the carvings. "Here this is all I need to do to make people believe I am real. To make them comfortable."

"Smoke and mirrors," Alex said.

"Literal smoke and mirrors," Selah agreed.

"But once they are here; do you know how many times my gift has allowed me to make a change?" A girl changes her major and SHE can make the laws. A boy who is suicidal gets the hope he needs to try again. A man who is considering running away goes home to his family. These changes," she tapped her finger on the table for emphasis, "they are as real as any of that."

After years of watching her friend work, Alex had to agree.

But now her friend was watching her. "You wanna talk about it?" Selah asked.

Alex shook her tawny tresses. "Not right now. I'll wait until everyone is here. I... I don't think that I can go through it all twice."

Selah didn't push. That was one of the best things about her; she never pushed. She was, however, obviously concerned.

"But you're all right?" she asked.

"No," Alex said simply. "I'm not hurt, but I'm not all right. I will be, though."

Selah nodded, satisfied, and hugged Alex once again. Alex turned and walked through the swinging door that led to Selah's back room. It was her kitchen and break room all in one; she lived in the apartment above the salon, and it was like walking into a different world. The walls were a nondescript sand-color, and three mismatched and rump-sprung couches crowded for position around a battle-scarred coffee table. The coffee table was currently supporting a pair of boots that, in turn, led to Dave Hartsell. Dave was a local bicycle messenger. He was under heavy demand, being greatly favored for his quicker-than-average delivery time, no matter the weather or traffic. That was his gift; he was able to discern the quickest route to any address, whether he had been there before or not. Alex called out a greeting and he nodded noncommittally. Acerbically witty and silent as the grave he may be, he was actually rather sweet and devoted to the small amount of people he considered friends. He had long hair and an equally long nose, that was generally pointed downwards towards his cell phone. He was on the phone at that very moment, smirking at something that he read. In real life, Dave was incredibly shy and an introvert the likes of which Alex had never seen. Hearing five words during their lunches was rare. However, he was something of an online celebrity due to a persona he had developed on Reddit and other such sites. Alex had read some of his posts and she could certainly see the appeal. It was surreal, though, consolidating the bombastic personae with her quiet friend.

"Tinder?" she teased. His teeth flashed, and Alex settled onto a couch with a sigh, massaging her temples. That was a mistake; every time she closed her eyes for any length of time, the images from that morning flashed through her head. The breasts, the moaning, the hotel. Alex sat up sharply.

"Dave!" she nearly yelled.

Dave raised his head. His dark brows were furrowed.

"If I described the inside of a building, could you find it?" He thought about it for a moment, tapping his fingers on his thigh.

"I dunno," he said at last, "I've never tried. Why?"

Alex started to reply when the back door flew open. A stream of profanity flowed into the room, followed by the familiar smell of cigarette smoke and body odor combined with ginger and garlic.

"Hola, motherfuckers," Vinnie shouted by way of greeting.

Foul-mouthed and abrasive was Vinnie's baseline. In fact, he had a habit of referring to himself, impulsively and apropos of nothing, as a "genuine New York Dago," and affectation that never failed to make his companions cringe. Much of Vinnie's humor made them cringe, truth be told, but still they loved him. Vinnie could speak to pigeons, only pigeons, which combined with his temper had led to his exodus from New York. As Pasha had once said, a gift like Vinnie's limited his choices to abrasive jerk or altruistic Pollyanna, and Vinnie would never be able to pull off the braids.

"Hello, Vinnie," Dave replied mildly.

Alex tapped her fingernails restlessly on her knee. She was hoping to talk more with Dave about the hotel, he was bit forgetful, but she pushed it aside. She needed to center, and more than that, have a plan before she went home, and these people were the only ones she knew who could help her with both. Alex rose and gave Vinnie the customary kiss on the cheek as Selah entered, letting in a whiff of pan flute and incense.

"Pasha?" she asked, looking at the clock.

"Fashionably late," Alex replied. "As usual," Vinnie added with a snort of laughter. It was true, the group had started factoring "Pasha time" into their plans years before.

"I say we start," Vinnie said, "I'm fucking starving."

Sure enough, Alex was barely two bites into her lo Mein when Pasha came through the front door, pulling the beaded curtain aside with a look that was equal parts nonchalance and wry humor. He looked dapper as always in a wide-brimmed hat, tapered coat, and a silk scarf. It was, Alex knew, a look tailored more for functionality than fashion though it was well suited to both. Direct sunlight was, for Pasha, incredibly painful.

"That scarf is amazing," Alex said as Pasha sat, helping himself to his container of dumplings.

It really was beautiful, painted in watercolors the hues of the sunset. Alex found that, now that the moment she had been waiting for, the moment she could unload the weight of the past nine hours was here, she was hesitant, ashamed. Almost as if she was the one who had done something wrong. She looked for a way to delay.

"Where did you get it?" she asked.

"Here," Pasha replied, tossing it to her, "take it."

Alex caught the soft material, and he boldly waved her protests away.

"It's fine, love. It's one of Blaine's designs. A new client. There's more where that came from."

"Client?" Selah asked with a raised eyebrow. Pasha blushed, a physiological feat that always mystified Alex.

"He's also a client."

"Pasha!" Alex exclaimed. "He's like, what? One quarter your age?"

"Everybody is at this point," he replied. "Besides, as far as anyone knows I'm an incredibly well-preserved 40."

"Bitch," Vinnie muttered.

"Cretin," Pasha replied in his softly accented voice. "Why don't you ask your birds to bring you some class?"

Everyone laughed. That exchange, or one just like it, had taken place at every lunch for years. The two gentlemen argued like brothers but were, underneath it all, very fond of one another. Pasha had found a way for Vinnie to have some regular work, his demeanor combined with his gift made employment difficult, and once Vinnie had gotten a lead on a swanky downtown loft that Pasha had been coveting, when his pigeons passed on some gossip about adultery and divorce. Alex picked at her food, letting the banter flow around her.

She was so lost inside her own head that she didn't notice the silence when it grew.

"Alex," Selah said softly, her hands on Alex's arms. Alex jumped.

"What? I'm sorry," she said.

"Dave just asked you a question, sweetie."

"Can you tell me more about the building you want me to find?" he repeated. Alex chewed her lower lip.

"It's more than that," she said quietly. "Guys… I need your help."

Slowly, haltingly, she told them what happened, her face flushed with shame. They reacted with outrage, and compassion, exactly what she needed. They did not, however, react with shock and she made a mental note to ask more about that later. Dave suggested that she go to the police, but even as they said it, they knew it wouldn't work. She had earned a place in the force, had even been called upon as an expert witness, but this one was a whole different game. Even if the D.A. believed her, which was doubtful without more to back it up, she didn't just want to live through the next few weeks; she wanted to never have to be afraid again. She wanted Neil to pay. To do that, she would have to know more. Vinnie offered to sic the pigeons on him.

"Thanks, Vinnie," she laughed through her tears, "but I think that might tip him off to something."

"You laugh," Selah said, suddenly somber, "but it's true; it's imperative that he not know that anything is different. If he suspects, he could clean out the accounts… or worse."

"I personally feel like the accounts are the least of your worries, but if you give me your permission I'll take care of them. I have all of your information," said Pasha.

Alex lowered her head, but nodded.

"Selah," Pasha shuddered a bit, "and loathe as I am to say it, Vinnie, are right, though Alex, you have to make sure he doesn't suspect. This man is dangerous."

"Are you up to it?" Selah asked Alex.

"I guess I'll have to be," Alex replied.

"Can you?"

Alex nodded. "I think I can, knowing you all are there. I really think I can."

*   *   *

ALEX dawdled in the back room, researching the professor whose makeshift shrine she had visited earlier while her friends left, one by one. Dave went to go make deliveries that were due before the end of business day, with a promise that he would get to work on identifying the hotel. Pasha slipped out after wrapping himself tightly against the sun and lovingly bullying

Alex into a promise of a dinner date the next night. Vinnie, surprisingly, stayed the longest and would not leave until she'd accepted protection. Alex was wary, unsure if it would be a flock of pigeons or Vinnie himself who would be tailing her, and even less sure about what her preference would be. Finally, though, she relented, and he left with a very un-Vinnie like hug. Selah came back between appointments until her face confirmed what Alex's frequent glimpses at her phone had already suggested – it was time to go.

"You know what I'm going to say," Selah said. Alex nodded as she stood.

"I don't know how I'm going to do this."

"Because you are a strong, smart, incredible woman."

Alex nodded. There were no tears to bite back; her day had accomplished that much at least. "Yes, but I still don't know..."

"I do," Selah replied.

"How's that?"

"Because I know how much you want to live."

"Selah?" Alex asked. Her friend looked at her attentively. "You know how I said to never use your gift on me?" Selah nodded. "I take it back, for now. If there's something you see, something you think I need to hear, tell me." The taller woman chuckled.

"I always do. Not because of my gift. Because I'm your friend."

Chapter Five

ALEX could see the lights from her house as she came down her block and her heart sank; regardless of her assurances to Selah, she was still not 100% certain that she could perform on this level. She took two deep, steadying breaths and opened the door. Alex had just enough time to see the deli tray sitting on the bar, three different cheeses, prosciutto, olives, before Neil came out of the bedroom, a slim gun held in his right hand. Alex gasped and started to dive behind the counter in the split second before she recognized that the gun was, in fact, the newest smartphone in its waterproof case. Alex reacted quickly, but, it appeared, not quickly enough. Neil had noticed and approached her with a look suspended between concern and laughter.

"What the hell was that about?" he asked.

Somewhere inside Alex's brain, a tiny little man started flipping through the files marked "witty response," but came up double zero. She tried "surefire distractions" with the same result. Alex's heart started to pound even faster, knowing that she may have come close to raising suspicions right out of the gate.

"It's been..." she started and trailed off. There was a red smudge on his collar.

"What? It's been what, Alex?" he asked.

"A long day," she finished lamely.

It was a pathetic answer, she knew it was pathetic, but either Neil allowed compassion to obscure suspicion or he didn't care enough to press further. Alex suspected the latter, but still he folded her into a hug.

"The wild world of computer security," he teased, "danger lurking around every corner."

*   *   *

ALEX hadn't meant to lie to Neil about what she did for a living, at least not long-term. She did on their first date and then, when things got more serious, she kept meaning to come clean, but an appropriate time never came. Then, too much time, and too many snarky comments had passed and so the lie had spun out. For the first time, she was grateful.

"You have no idea," she said. "Some scammer was trying to make a client's website direct to his own."

"Woah," he replied, a fake tremor in his voice. "And what did he sell?"

"Used underpants." Alex had no idea why that came out. Vinnie had once enthralled and terrified them with tales of what was a surprisingly lively and lucrative business, and it must have stuck somewhere in her mind. Still, as a distraction, it seemed to work as Neil let the matter drop, turning away with a chuckle and pouring her a drink. Gin. She hated gin.

"Drink this," he said, bringing it to her, "for medicinal reasons."

A couple of glasses later, he headed to bed, taking Alex by the hand as he led the way. At the bathroom door, Alex paused.

"I'll be right there." She kissed him lightly on the lips, her head tucking against his chest. She walked away, gazing deeply into his eyes, and closed the door behind her as he continued down the hall. Then, she picked up the onyx and stared at it, chewing on her lower lip. She knew that she shouldn't put it on. She knew that she needed to go into the next few days with her eyes, all of them, wide open. Yet she fastened the onyx around her neck. For one night, she would take her chances. Tomorrow she could be scared and angry. She could be a detective. Tomorrow she could be a psychic. For just one night, for her last night, she just wanted to be a wife.

The lights were out when she entered the room, the bed illuminated just slightly by the streetlights streaming in between the blinds and through the gauzy curtains. She saw Neil's eyes glittering in the dark, the white flash of his smile. With a squeezing pain that felt like a goodbye, choking back a sob, Alex climbed into bed beside him. He was aroused, naked, and powerfully hard. Alex trailed a line of kisses that started at his stomach and traveled downward until her tongue flicked at the base of his penis. She licked his shaft, tracing the lines and ridges of him with her tongue, teasing him, smiling as he grabbed the sheets and thrust his hips upward. She pulled back the first time, keeping her tongue flicking while she moved her lips just out of reach, but when he thrust again she took him in fully, moaning at the smell, the feel, the taste of him. One of her hands curled around the base of his shaft while the other slid under her panties, to the cleft where she was already wet. Let other people roll their eyes, a good blowjob was always as much for her as it was for the man she was with, and with just a few strokes at the silky nub between her legs Alex came, her throat tightening against the head of Neil's member. He grabbed her under her arm then flipping her onto her back and moving her up the bed in one smooth move, ripping her shirt open to stroke her breasts. Visions tried to work their way into Alex's mind, even through the onyx. A jewelry box opening, a dark cave, but Alex willed them out. Tonight was hers and his. With a groan of passion, almost a growl, Alex threw her legs around Neil's waist and locked her ankles. She was kissing him so hard that their teeth clicked, over and over and she knew that their lips would be swollen in the morning. He slid into her, his eyes closed. "Look at me," she gasped, and he did. They rocked together until he emptied himself into her and Alex fell asleep, one last time, peacefully in the arms of her husband.

*   *   *

FOR a brief moment the next morning, lying there sated and comfortable, Alex thought that maybe, just maybe, she had been wrong about the whole thing. Neil had no time for infidelity; he was hardly the flirtatious or schmoozy type. And murder? That was ridiculous. She was mistaken, that was all. Granted, she hadn't been wrong since she learned to control her gift, but it could happen. She held on to that daydream for exactly as long as it took for her to open her eyes. Neil's suitcase lay open on top of the dresser, three days' worth of clothes folded neatly, of course, inside. Her heart dropped for a moment, but only a moment before her detective's mind, honed and sharpened carefully over the years, kicked in. Sorrow, rage, even love, anything she felt or had felt for Neil was once again shoved into a box, the door slammed on it, to be dealt with later. That it would have to be dealt with, she knew, but for now, the watertight doors held. As such, when Alex kissed Neil goodbye, she was able to do so with a dry eye and a smile that seemed almost genuine.

*   *   *

ALEX left shortly after Neil did. Her files and laptop were neatly tucked in her overnight bag. She headed for Common Grounds, where the barista, a twenty-something with a septum piercing almost as large as Alex's pinkie and myriad tattoos had her order ready by the time Alex got to the front of the line. "Hey, you're back!" Alex exclaimed.

The barista grinned back, "and you didn't even have to release me." The young girl, Raven, was one of the few people in Louisville who put her political money where her mouth was, travelling as far as her money would allow to attend protests, volunteering at the local homeless shelter, fostering dogs for the local shelter. There was little that she didn't do. When Alex had walked into the sheriff's office just as she and a group of others were in-processed, she had called in all the favors owed by those in the force and otherwise to advocate for and win their release.

"Maybe next time," Alex grabbed her mega tall mocha funky monkey, topped with so much whipped cream that it nearly collapsed. Raven knew of her childlike affinity for the stuff, and never failed to indulge her.

She headed to her usual spot, a table and chair that were close to both the window and the speaker, before she realized how exposed she was. Furrowing her brow, she moved, nothing it seemed was going to be mundane for a while. Alex headed to the back of the shoppe, where she could not be seen from the outside, but had a view of the entire space. She stared at the table for a minute, wondering if it was strong enough to stop a bullet if needs be, before sitting down. After an hour of study, she knew that there was nothing that she could glean from the professor. For such a beloved member of the community, he had left very little tangible legacy. He had neither spouse nor children, had rented an apartment, and even his office was already occupied by his successor. Alex shut his file with a sigh and opened the next. The second victim had been SPC Tony Grant. Grant had left the military on full disability and with a Purple Heart after losing part of his leg in a Humvee accident overseas. He had come home a reluctant hero, and moved back in with his parents. She found the parents' home number, and after taking a moment to consider, she detested having to bother grieving families, she dialed. Grant's mother was kind if weary and agreed to allow Alex to come over that afternoon, with the caveat that she be gone by five. "His father," the woman explained apologetically, "he hasn't handled this well and I'd rather he didn't have a...

reminder." Alex gave her word and hung up. There were two text messages waiting.

The first was from Selah, making sure that she was okay, and the second was Pasha confirming their plans for that evening. Alex replied to both, her thumbs flying over the letters. Shortly after 10:30, Raven left, shouting a goodbye to Alex on her way out the door. By the time Alex closed the files two hours later, she could recite the names, ages, and any other relevant information about all of the victims. They ran the gamut in age, race, and socioeconomic status. In fact, there was nothing at all that connected them, at least on the surface, other than the gun used to end their lives.

*　　　*　　　*

WHEN Alex reached SPC Grant's home, she had nearly given herself whiplash constantly looking over her shoulder. Still, with a roll of her shoulders, Alex compartmentalized that part of her life and was able then to meet the soldier's mother with a smile that was both warm and appropriately somber. Grant's mother escorted her to the victim's room, her face bore the marks of too much pain experienced too quickly. She left without looking in. Gently, Alex closed the door.

SPC Grant's room had remained untouched since his death, save the not-quite-precise rummaging of the police, it had the feel of incomplete transition. A young boy's poster of baseball heroes hung across from snapshots of broad shouldered and dirt-coated young men and women in uniform.

A video game console shared space with newspapers on the desk. Looking around, Alex slid some earbuds in and thumbed through a playlist called, simply, "sexy." She closed her eyes picturing... who? As ridiculous as it may seem to some, Neil had never been her fantasy man. She flipped through the mental rolodex of men she used for psychic inspiration, but none seemed to get her attention. "Let's Dance," the Thin White Duke crooned in her ear. That did it. It usually did, and Alex's hands started to buzz lightly. She walked around the room, feeling for something, anything. She approached the guitar in the corner and caught a flash – a bonfire, the light flickering golden on the faces around it and a sweet buzzing in the vein. Two steps closer and there was another one, a wide-eyed blonde lying naked while the young man sang. She could feel the images building, one after another, when her phone rang, jerking her out of her mental space. The images dissolved. She was unable to hide the frustration in her voice as she barked into the phone.

"Campbell," Hank sounded strained, slightly out of breath. "There's been another murder. We think it's the same guy. If you hurry, you may get something." Alex left, after murmuring an apology to Grant's mother, asking permission to send some officers by to collect the guitar as evidence. She sent a text to Pasha, cancelling their plans, chugged an energy drink and pulled up to the curb so fast that her tires squealed. By the time she made it across town, the area had been cordoned off with yellow tape and black and whites were parked blocking a small alley. Hank met her on the street and escorted her to the scene.

"Are you sure this is one of ours?" Alex asked.

"No," Hank replied, "All that we know now is that it is a GSW, large caliber. I thought I'd call you out anyway, just in case." He put one hand on the small of her back, steadying her as she stepped over an upended trashcan and dodged around another. They maneuvered around two other officers blocking her view and she stopped short and gasped, one hand to her mouth. There, her black combat boot splayed in a V, a third red eye glaring sightless at the sky just as the other two were, lay Raven.

Chapter Six

ALEX cried. She hated it, especially in front of so many street-hardened cops. She hated crying at all, ever, and it seemed like in the last few days that was all that she had done. Still, she couldn't help it. Raven had been her friend. She explained as much to Hank, his arm around her shoulders. He passed the information quickly to the other uniforms, then hurried back to her side. She thought then about telling him what she had seen inside of Neil. A small, self-loathing filled part of her brain was convinced that it was that that had led to Raven's death, and not the other. Still, somehow that didn't feel right, and she didn't want to muddy the waters. "Also, you don't want to face the humiliation," the inner voice interjected. "Shut up," Alex replied. She didn't realize that she had said that out loud until Hank turned, looked at her quizzically. "Sorry," she said feebly. He put his hands on her shoulders and peered deep into her eyes. As the icy blue orbs bored into hers, Alex could feel herself center.

"Can you go on?" Alex nodded, smiling weakly. "All right then; let's get this done." He hugged her again and Alex inhaled, luxuriating in the scent of his cologne.

Her gift needed surprisingly little coaxing. Hank's smell still echoed in her head, as did the strength of his arms, and

Alex mentally painted them on her favorite celebrity crush. She was on a beach on the coast, pulling his pirate coat away from his intensely sculpted abs. She felt the warmth that started in the pit of her stomach and coiled downward into her private eye. Alex walked in a slow spiral starting at the body. At first there was nothing. Then, about ten yards from the body, Raven's body, she got something. A sickly, brown-tinged green. Feelings of what? Pride? Lust? Alex couldn't tell; it was all jumbled together, but it was strong. Alex tracked it, the color trailing in front of her for blocks. Other colors, other feelings, interrupted occasionally, but she was able to focus in until she found herself across the street from "The Office," the pseudo-upscale "Gentleman's Club" that had occupied its same location since prohibition and now sat incongruously between a parking garage and a gourmet burger restaurant. There, his trail merged with so many others that, though she could feel it from yards away, it blurred. "There," she said to Hank, pointing, "he's in there."

"Can you do better than that?" Hank asked. "There will be dozens of guys in there, maybe more."

Alex thought about it, then shook her head. "Not now, maybe with some time, but I won't be able to sort him from the others right away. Not without sex." Hank did a brief double take and blushed a bit, then his jaw worked in frustration and he stared at the club as if trying to glare through the walls. Finally, he turned away.

"Let's go then," he said. They waited until the coroner had loaded the body and then she followed him to the precinct. Her route to the bullpen for Hank's case meeting was suddenly blocked by the overpowering stench of Bath and Bubble

Shoppe and a pair of breasts. Alex had never thought of breasts as a barricade until she had to dodge the navy-clad pair, thrust out and up with some torture device the likes of which she had never imagined.

"Excuse me," Alex said, and tried to move around the breasts and the woman behind them. She hated Bath and Bubble Shoppe. It reminded her of her step-mother; the monster that her father had married when she was barely ten and whose constant stream of lowbrow abuse had driven her from his house and into her grandmother's time and time again and eventually, for good.

"Ms. Campbell," a voice drawled, low and commanding, "we need to talk."

One half-hour later Alex sat in the office that, last time she had graced the interior, belonged to Captain Jeffries, a curmudgeonly old vet who tolerated no touchy-feelies but was a true advocate for both his officers and his victims. Jeffries had retired two months before, after his third heart attack. While Alex had heard rumbles about the new Captain Lobe, (whose nickname Frontal Lobe suddenly made so much more sense), this was the first time that she had made her acquaintance. As she focused on a point in between the captain's eyes, letting her face blur and soften, Alex felt herself losing the ability to endure much more of the lecture that she had been receiving, with no break, for thirty minutes. The guitar, apparently, had been a mistake. "What authority do you have," Captain Lobe had begun, "ordering my officers to run your errands?" Alex had started to respond but had gotten no further than to open her mouth before the Captain had steamrolled right over her. Alex had not tried again. A change in tone signaled to Alex that the tirade, or, more accurately, the ass-chewing, was complete. "Now, Captain Jeffries approved of your..."her lip coiled into a sneer, "methods, and Detective Barnett speaks highly of you. I have also been assured that what you do is not technically prostitution, no matter how much it may seem so to me." Alex clenched her jaw so hard that she could feel her teeth cracking, but she could not control the flush in her cheeks. The smug look in the Captain's eyes twinkled as though she had won an argument, and she continued, "and so I will allow you to stay on retainer. However, while you are here you obey my rules; do you understand?"

Alex breathed deep for a moment and swallowed hard, literally forcing down words that she desperately and furiously wanted to say. When she spoke, however, her voice was clear and even if a bit sharper than that she generally used. "Yes, Captain."

"Good. You're dismissed." Suddenly, Captain Lobe's face diffused with color. Her eyes widened, her mouth opened and the harsh angles of her face rounded. For a moment, Alex actually thought that the vile woman was having a stroke. Then, the door creaked, and Alex could smell the spice of Hank's cologne. He stood in the doorway, joined by Sergeant DuPre. Alex did not like Sergeant DuPre. He was a lofty know-it-all combined with the cowering grin of the Beta male. He always seemed to be busy doing a whole lot of nothing. She also hated the tiny little moustache inching along his upper lip. It looked like a caterpillar. An undernourished one. It didn't take her long to understand another layer of the dynamic into which she had fallen, the muddle of pheromones pouring out of Captain Lobe were enough that Alex's senses detected a bit of exhaustion, and stress. Not enough for her to feel compassion after the treatment she had just received, but some.

"Captain Lobe, I wanted to thank you for your help on this case." The captain didn't respond, though her jaw tightened and raised a bit. "The guitar. I think it could really lead us somewhere. Thank you for allowing the Sergeant here to secure it while I was busy." To her credit, Alex noted, the Captain had too much pride and professionalism to either simper or argue.

"Of course,' she said. "Happy to do it." Alex's eyed widened and her head snapped to Hank. He nodded almost imperceptibly.

"May I take Miss Campbell off your hands?" he asked.

"I wish you would," the Captain replied. "Miss Campbell," she called out as Alex reached the door, and Alex turned reluctantly. "I look forward to not having to speak with you again."

"Me as well," Alex said, not worrying about how the woman might take it, and allowed Hank to close the door behind her. She exhaled and pushed back the tendrils of hair that had worked their way out of her twist and into her eyes. They walked in silence until DuPre hooked a right down a hallway, whistling tunelessly under his breath.

"Drink?" Hank asked. Alex nodded vigorously.

"Please."

*   *   *

THE Seven Dwarves was dark and cozy, precisely what Alex needed. It was a Louisville staple, nestled underneath the myriad underpasses that made up spaghetti junction and featured dark wood, craft beers and amazing food. Best of all, there was only one door and no real windows to speak of, which explained its popularity among police officers as well as down town office workers and hipsters eager to sample their craft beers. The waitress seated them at a booth and while Hank excused himself Alex returned his favor from the other day and ordered for the both of them, remembering his preferences from years of easy friendship. The drinks arrived at the same time that Hank did, and he raised one beautifully sculpted eyebrow at the bourbon porter, so dark it looked black.

"You're gonna have to chew that more than your meal," he said.

Alex rolled her eyes, then nodded at the pale gold that filled his glass. "Save it," she teased, "with what I just spent on that I could've bought a case of Natty Light and I don't think you could have told the difference."

"Touché." Hank sat and drank, deftly flicking at the foam on his lip.

Something south of Alex's breasts gave a shiver. "What the hell is wrong with me today?" she thought. "So, the Captain," she began pointedly.

"The Captain," he repeated with a sigh and finished the rest of his glass. The waitress brought another and this time around, he began. Alex was not surprised to find that the woman had been a nightmare since day one. More interested in politics than policework, she had transferred in from an administrative role at headquarters and, though her office had moved, her loyalties hadn't. The officers were being forced to justify every decision, every unit worked overtime. "That woman has taken CYA to a new level." Hank muttered. Once his words had begun, they'd flowed out in a torrent, and it didn't take Selah's form of clairvoyance to discern that he had needed this for a long time. Clearly, rising through the ranks in an admittedly male-dominated world, the testosterone had driven Alex insane repeatedly, couldn't be easy for the Captain. Still, the woman seemed determined to make all the men in the precinct pay for the insults of those who had come before. And they were the lucky ones. The men she looked to put in their place; the women she despised. So much so that two of the three female officers had put in requests to transfer. The third, a battle-hardened Amazon had taken to carrying entire bottles of Tums in her back pocket and the tell-tale streaks of white powder were collecting at the corners of her mouth.

"She scared off the Angels?" Alex exclaimed. The trio of women of the station had gone briefly viral a year before, when a picture of them coolly facing down a local drug lord and his small gang of armed thugs made it to the internet. Hank nodded. "The thugs you could at least reason with." Alex signaled for another round, "And now she hates me." Hank took his lower lip in his teeth, pondering, and it slid back to fullness slowly, glistening. The waitress' return cut short Alex's appreciation of the visual, and by the time the woman had left, empty glasses in tow, Alex had composed herself.

"She hates the idea of you, I think," Hank said at last. "Beautiful, hyper-intelligent, respected by the force — which she isn't — and unapologetic about who you are and what you do."

"You'd think she'd approve of at least the last part," Alex said.

Hank shook his head. "Nah, she uses her gender like a weapon. You, you're something different. Special. We see it, and she does too." Their gaze held perhaps a beat longer than was necessary before Alex spoke again.

"About that girl today — the victim," she began, then paused at the look of warning that crossed his face. He rubbed at the muscles at the back of his neck.

"Can it wait, Alex," he asked. "If it can't tell me, but, can it wait until tomorrow? I'm fried." Alex thought about it. She had been about to tell him about her relationship with Raven, why she felt guilty for the girl's death even though she was sure the two weren't connected. Well, almost sure. She'd see what she discovered as she dove deeper in. Maybe then she would be sure.

In the meantime, "Yeah," she said, "It can wait." She knew she'd be opening a bigger can of worms than she wanted to anyway. Would have to explain the rest of the story, Neil's affair, the suspected assassin, the inconvenience and fear of it all. She'd rather take her chances.

*   *   *

THEY finished their drinks in a companionable almost-silence, and Alex took a minute to change the code on her locks using her phone, an act which made her simultaneously curse and stand in awe of technology. Arriving home, she got out of her car, keys and shoes dangling from one hand, and shoving the other into the specially made pocket of her purse, feeling the cool steel of the weapon that she'd bought over a decade earlier and kept up to practice with on the range. She realized then that she was out of hands, and stuffed her phone down the front of her shirt. Eyes darting around, hand still on her weapon, she set her shoes on the porch and used her phone to open the door. Carefully, warily, she searched every room, only putting her purse down with a sigh of relief when every one proved clean. Exhausted and with no further ado, Alex disrobed and climbed gratefully into bed.

Though her mind was fuzzy, her body buzzed, Alex grumbled and rolled from one side to another. She stretched her long leg towards the foot of the bed then relaxing, tightening the muscles so that they'd stop twitching and she could sleep. It didn't work. She was jumping, adrenaline pumping into her system with every bump, every hiss in the house. She never noticed how many noises there were before. The buzzing was getting more insistent. She knew the cure for this. More irritated than aroused, but desperate to do something, Alex rolled onto her back and parted her legs. Usually on nights like this Alex was all business, three minutes, do these things in this order, the brain releases the right chemical and orgasm was achieved, no fantasy required. Sufficient if not entirely satisfying. This time, though, as her finger touched the top of her cleft and she felt the first jolt of electricity burst through her body Hank's face, his shy grin, swam before her eyes. Years. For years they'd been working together. Partners in crime. At least, partners in crime-solving.

She'd even set him up on more than one date, to varying degrees of success. With the end of her marriage, and possibly her life, looming it was as if a door, one that had been so thoroughly closed that she didn't know it existed, was rattling in its frame. Alex's hand, meanwhile, worked on its own until she rattled in her frame. She rubbed the delicate ball of nerves in slow circles then fast, faster, every nerve on her body woke fully. The tension built more and more until finally, as she pictured removing Hank's belt and sliding her hands down his pants, she plunged two fingers deep inside herself and finished. Three minutes later, Alex was fast asleep.

Chapter Seven

ALEX was up and out of the house by 6:30. Two pigeons cooed sleepily from their roost on her porch. They took off in a litter of gray and white feathers and a splat of droppings that narrowly missed her head. She cursed. At the pigeons, at the dawn, at the existence of a world before 8. She hated mornings, tried not to greet them fully unless she had to do so, but she figured that it would help prolong her life a little bit if she varied her routine. Also, she had an appointment with Hank and was desperate to get to the station before Frontal Lobe. A light feather brushed against Alex as she shut the door and she jumped a bit before looking down guiltily. In the soft light of pre-morning, the bright angles of her skirt nearly glowed. Resistance through ruffles, she thought wryly. Her first outfit of the day had been one of her most bland, conservative; a pair of black-wide-legged trousers with a little button-down blouse. There was no reason to draw attention to herself. After a moment's consideration, though, Alex realized, that yes, yes there was damn well a reason. She had no reason for shame, and if the Captain was so determined to focus on only her femininity, that was what she would get. Alex had rummaged to the back of her closet and picked out a heavily flowered, brightly printed dress that she'd bought on impulse in Key

West and never had the chance to wear once she got out of the Conch Republic. Gauzy, flowy, and ruffled, it was the epitome of girliness. Alex loved it. She laughed and slipped it over her head and had been giggling on and off ever since. Resistance through Roses. Viva la fleurs!

*   *   *

THE uniform at the front table did a double-take when she arrived, trying to keep a straight face but failing, his lips curving beneath his neatly trimmed moustache. "All right," he said approvingly. Alex stepped inside the inner sanctum, checked the guitar out of evidence, and settled herself in the gray carpeted conference room. She adjusted her bracelet, and closed her eyes, focusing on the energy from the day before. It returned slowly. Alex rummaged in her purse and put in her earbuds. Flicking through her playlist, soon electric synthesizers of the 1980s blasted in her ear and her mind filled with images of shirtless young men playing volleyball on beaches, flexing their glistening muscles when they checked their watches. That would do it as it did for almost any straight women born in the '80s. The scenes started to flow again. A break up with the girl who had said yes, a hospital, onstage at dingy bars, finally, surrounded by uniforms in a dusty foreign land. Then, the images petered out and Alex propped her chin on her cheek, staring into nothingness. Such promise, such heartbreak, then even that cut short. She noticed the time and began to quickly scramble her stuff together. The bullpen meeting was starting in 20 minutes, and she needed another coffee. "People at the bar?" she scrawled into her notebook, "drugs? Military?" She returned the guitar then headed to the coffee machine. The brew was dark, bitter, cop-strength and the powdered creamer was about 5 years out of date, but it was something. Thus armed, she strode into the bullpen. She had known that her appearance would not go unnoticed, and it hadn't. What she did not expect was how far word had spread. As each officer passed through the room, they handed her a piece of fruit purchased from the tiny commissary. Soon, her lap was full of bananas, oranges, even tiny plastic cups of pineapple. Alex took the ribbing good-naturedly, even gratefully, fully aware that it was a genuine if warped sign of solidarity. Hank arrived, three minutes early as usual, showing no outward sign of the frustration he'd shown the night before.

"DuPre here?" he asked. The others shook their heads.

"Hear he may have needed a lobotomy," one of them said. Hank's eyes flashed, and the officer muttered an apology. His eyes flashed towards the Captain's office.

"We can't wait," Hank said. "Let's move this to my office." Even with only four officers in addition to Hank and Alex, the small room was cramped. Hank caught the other officers up quickly and concisely. There, his frustration did show, if only through the throbbing of his veins and the whiteness of his lips, and Alex's eyes widened slightly, impressed at how quickly the others went from playful to professional. Eventually, Hank's brief ended, and Alex stepped in, sharing what she had discovered. She started with the possible leads she'd gotten from the guitar. Hank assigned two of his officers, a duo named Miggs and Tash who inevitably went by Mash, to follow up. After that, they moved on to the tracking that she had done, the greenish hue that led her to The Office. While people seemed energized at some sort of a lead, any sort, they were at a bit of a loss.

"We could interview some of the dancers?" someone suggested.

Hank shook his head. "We don't want to tip him off. Also, we don't have anything concrete to ask them to look for. He wouldn't have blood on him, and even though our profile is woefully incomplete, I doubt he's bragging about his conquests."

"How about surveillance," another cop asked.

"For what?" Hank asked. "Shady dudes going into a strip club? Guys I'm not trying to shoot you down, but you know Lobe is going to need us to justify any move we make. Let's make good ones."

"Well," said Miggs, "I am personally willing to stay there as long as it takes to pick up any sort of hint," The rest snickered at this, bantering back and forth.

"You are going up on the pole, Mash," they asked.

"I'd be happy to stick a dollar in your thong."

"A dollar?" Miggs roared in indignation, flexing his arms, "These alone are worth more than that." The bullpen erupted in groans and catcalls. They were so loud that Alex wasn't heard the first time she spoke up.

"I'll do it," she said. She cleared her throat and tried again. "I'll do it," she repeated. "I'll go undercover and see if I can find something out." The silence started out at absolute and deepened as the officers realized exactly what she meant. One officer fidgeted, another rubbed his lip and looked away.

"Miss Campbell," Tash began, his drawl thick, "I don't doubt that you'd do just fine... investigatin'. But The Office ain't your average," he grasped for words, "Mammary establishment." The room exploded again, Hank facepalmed with an audible smack.

"What my partner is trying to say is that's it's dangerous, ma'am."

"He has a point, Alex, no social skills, but a point. We get called down there all the time. Assault, narcotics—"

"All the more reason we need to end this quickly," Alex interrupted. Hank didn't answer. "Y'all I've been in a," she cut her eyes playfully at Miggs, enunciating carefully, "gentleman's club before." She could tell that they still weren't convinced. She was torn between gratitude for and irritation with their concern. She was, after all, hardly a damsel in distress. If that was what they wanted, however... Alex slumped, lowering her lashes and pursing her lips. She sighed deeply and then straightened up. Sad but strong. It had the desired effect; she had their undivided attention. "If it makes you feel any better," she began, "You'll be doing me a favor as well." Slowly, with a haltingness that was not part of her show, Alex explained what she had discovered and how. They reacted just as she had thought they would, with a protectiveness that made her glad that she wasn't the perpetrator. She waded through the prerequisite offers to "disappear him" and "take his place" and when they had died down she continued. "The way I see it, we'd be doing each other a solid. I'd be somewhere that he couldn't find me, and you'd have someone who could follow this lead. As sexy as Miggs is," she continued, "I'm not sure he could pull off sequins." All eyes turned to Hank, whose jaw muscles bulged and relaxed as if he was chewing gum. Even through her onyx Alex could see deep crimson rolling off him. He stared at her for a long moment.

"All right," he said at last, "Let's do it. Alex, stay here. Let's get you what you need. The rest of you, get to work."

Hank leaned over his desk, his hands splayed on the scarred laminate. One foot tapping restlessly on the floor. He spoke in very measured tones. "Are you okay?" he said at last. Alex tried to answer. She tried several times but each time her resolve, her ability to compartmentalize shuddered with the weight of the water behind it.

"I'm surviving," she finally replied. Hank nodded slowly.

"Alex…"he said, and then nothing. "Why didn't you tell me?"

Alex picked at her cuticle for a moment. She'd always wanted model's hands, those well-manicured smooth wonders. But she couldn't handle the emotional burden of a manicure, the nail techs heard so much. So much and that emotion had to go somewhere. Her hands were large, blunt-tipped. "Because I didn't want this," she said at last.

"What?" Hank asked.

"This," Alex said louder, gesturing to the office. "I didn't want a dozen big brothers trying to protect me, getting in my way. I didn't want a bunch of people knowing my business, or a skeeze or two thinking this was their big break. I didn't want pity. I especially didn't want pity."

Hank moved to the front of his desk and put his hands lightly on her shoulders. She raised her eyes to his and shuddered a bit, remembering the night before. "I don't pity you," he said, "I pity him."

Alex felt rage start to rush through her then she caught Hank's smile. "In addition to being boring, and obviously stupid, if that man so much as hiccups in your direction he's going inside for years. "Alex laughed, a stray tear making its way down her cheek. "Probably has a small dick, too," he said as an afterthought.

"I've seen better," Alex agreed. Pettily. And it felt good. Indulging in her anger for a minute felt damn good.

"So, what do you need?" Hank asked.

Alex's mind worked rapidly. "I'll need a throwaway cell and a place to stay. Also, some identification. Some clothes. Do you have anyone in vice who could give me a primer?"

Hank nodded. "Yeah, and we will also get a couple of guys to show up every now and then, keep an eye on you, especially to and from work. When do you need this by?"

Alex pondered, "give me two days to get ready?" she asked.

Hank affirmed, "I'll also make sure you have some coverage between now and then."

Alex shook her head wordlessly, but Hank held up a hand.

"It's ultimately your call," he said, "but hear me out. I just want someone parked nearby, so if you need help, you just have to call. Otherwise we will stay out of your hair."

"If Captain Lobe finds out..." she began.

"Let me deal with her, please. Let me worry about that. You have enough." Alex thought about it, then nodded.

She stood then, arranging her dress, and stepped close to him, her arms raised. He hugged her, longer than usual then stepped away. His mouth worked as though he was trying to say something, but no words came.

"Thank you," she said evenly.

"No problem," he replied. "Anything else you need?"

"I think that's it," she said, holding his gaze.

He stepped closer. Just one step, a couple of inches, and electricity filled the air.

"Are you sure," he asked.

The silence spun out, and Alex cleared her throat. "I'll let you know," she said. He stepped back, his eyes holding hers.

"Stay safe then," he said.

Alex left, her heart pounding. Suddenly her life seemed very full.

Chapter Eight

ALEX met with Pasha that night after a trip to the local sex shop that Alex was in a bit of a hurry to forget. She had eschewed some of the swankier places, choosing the one closest to the station. She was no stranger to lingerie or toys, considered them perks of the job, in fact. Still, this place was something else altogether. A vast array of sexy whatever outfits here, everything from a nurse to school girls to cartoon characters. Mostly, though, it was porn, the likes of which even she had never imagined. She finally found what she was looking for, nestled in among gag gifts (no pun attended) and threadbare thongs in the clearance bin. She left with a "pole dancing for beginners" DVD and a sick feeling in the pit of her stomach.

Pasha walked in, late as usual, looking amazing. His suit was exquisitely cut and looked as if it had cost at least one month of her mortgage payment. His nails were freshly buffed, and he smelled delicious.

"Damn it Pasha," Alex said, kissing his cheek, "why are you always prettier than me?"

"Centuries of practice," he replied, pulling out her chair.

Alex looked around appraisingly. "You know, for someone who doesn't eat food for nourishment, you know some of the poshest places," she said.

"Anyone who eats for nourishment is a swine," he replied.

The dinner was amazing; local favorites like bourbon and fried chicken taken to a level that Alex had never imagined and she luxuriated in the flavors and Pasha's outrageous tales; stories of Pasha's new great love, Blaine, Vinnie's latest involuntary unemployment, all the easy banter that made Pasha one of Alex's favorite people from the first time they had met. As always, Alex laughed until her cheeks ached. Only when the plates were cleared, and the after-dinner cocktails poured did Pasha reach under his chair and pull two thin folders from his attaché. He passed one of them to Alex and they opened them in unison.

"I thought we would start with good news," Pasha said. "I have moved a sum of your assets into a trust and scheduled a series of deposits, small enough so that they won't be noticed, to continue. This trust will, naturally, be excluded from mutual property in the case of a divorce. I also, using methods I will not discuss, have provided enough to prove, if not that hitman, at least the affair."

"Pasha, you're amazing," she exclaimed. The vampire huffed a bit on his nails and pretended to polish their already glossy surface on a lapel. It was an act. Alex knew that he would no sooner muss his manicure than become a garlic farmer, but still she laughed. He smiled, but quickly it faded. He handed her another folder.

"And now for the bad news. As you can see, your joint savings account has been rather significantly depleted. Luckily you followed my advice and maintained an individual account. I took the liberty of moving a large chunk of the remainder of the joint account into some investments. The details are in your folder as well." Alex skimmed the withdrawals from the joint account. Hotels, jewelers, florists, hotels. A cruise.

"A cruise," she exclaimed, far louder than intended, and smiled a brief apology at the tables around her. "The motherfucker went on a cruise," she hissed.

Pasha reached out and squeezed her hand. "Yes," he said mildly, "the motherfucker did."

"How could he be so stupid to leave a trail like this," Alex marveled, eyeing the purchases.

"I don't think it was stupidity, love," Pasha said gently. "Just arrogance."

"He knew I didn't check that account much, and if I did he could explain it," Alex said.

"And you would believe him," Pasha agreed, "Or, he figured that before you could discover it the problem would resolve itself."

Alex massaged her temples. "Fine then, how could I be so stupid?" she asked.

"I don't think you were, either. You let me turn your business into an LLC, so he can't touch that. You bought your car and let him buy his—"

"—Both our suggestions," Alex said morosely. She gasped.

"You knew, didn't you," her eyes filled with tears of betrayal, "Pasha did you know? Do you have a magic vagina as well?"

Pasha shuddered. "Darling, I guarantee you that the words 'magic' and 'vagina' have never crossed my mind at the same time. I just suspected."

"But you barely knew him," she countered.

Pasha sighed heavily. "No, but I know the type. Always putting on a show, always the little digs towards you, the way he kept your worlds separate. I've met them before, guys like him."

"One of your exes?" Alex asked.

"No," Pasha replied. "One of theirs."

Alex's eyes widened. "Oooh," she said, "shall we pour the tea?"

Pasha looked at her with undisguised horror, "No, and please don't ever say that again, it doesn't suit you, darling. But, one night we will get very drunk on very good vodka, and I will tell you the story of beautiful, doomed, Vanya, my very first love."

"Why didn't you say anything?" Alex asked.

Pasha took rather longer than was necessary to wipe his mouth with his cloth napkin, then wet his lips and steepled his hands in front of his mouth, tapping his full lips. "Would you have believed us?" he countered, "You were so in love with him, so defensive of him. Vinnie once said that according to you he shot sunshine out of his ass when he farted." Pasha grimaced, "coarse as usual, but not inaccurate."

Alex's hands grew cold and she swallowed past sudden nausea.

"Oh, come here, love," Pasha said, pulling her into a hug. After a minute, he pulled away, and raised her chin gently with one finger. "So far you've tried to blame yourself and us. Maybe you should work the blame around to where it belongs," He booped the tip of her nose lightly.

Alex took a ragged breath and nodded. "Thank you," she said. "Pasha, can you do me a favor?" she asked.

"Anything," he said.

"If you see anything else that could protect my finances for the next couple of weeks, do it okay?" she said, "I'm going to be a little out of touch."

"Work?" he asked, one eyebrow dancing.

"Yeah," she replied.

"Will you be at Selah's salon?" he asked.

"No, but we will send word," she replied.

"Pigeons?" he asked.

"Pigeons," she confirmed, "and that's not the worst of it."

"Do tell," Pasha prompted as they headed towards the door.

"Somehow tomorrow, I have to go and sleep with my husband."

Chapter Nine

ALEX strutted into the offices of Roberts and Lewis. Her skirt clung to her legs, a good three inches higher than it usually did, and only barely containing her shapely ass. Her high heels, picked to make her legs look even longer, clicked on the tile in a manner that she found oddly satisfying. "Can I help you?" Marjorie, the myopic old battleax who had run the front desk for as long as anyone could remember, asked.

Alex flashed her a huge, fake smile. "No, thank you, Marjorie, I know where I'm going." Already pushing the up button on the elevator, Alex heard rather than saw the woman's sniff of disapproval. The harpy had hated her ever since the very first family cookout, for no good reason. It was, as far as Alex could tell, as purely a chemical reaction as she had ever seen. It used to bother Alex, and she had taken to sending cookies or plates of other treats by way of Neil. Gradually, she'd stopped being concerned, and today she couldn't have cared less. Just before the door closed, Alex saw Marjorie speaking quickly into the phone, and picked up a flash of the woman's panic. She knew, then, at least part of it. Innnnnnnnteresting.

Alex would have bet her last dollar that Marjorie had been calling up to Neil, and when she saw him standing in the hallway outside of his office, she knew that she would have come out of said bet a much wealthier woman. People walked up and down the corridor, speaking hurriedly into cell phones, or turned hurriedly into offices to start tapping away at their desks. Alex knew almost none of them. Though she hadn't lied to Marjorie, she knew where Neil's office was, she was far from familiar with the building and the workers, even though Neil had been there for more than a decade. Managment, Neil insisted, frowned upon family visits. They "did not contribute to productivity" and "compromised client security." The family cookouts and holiday parties decreased over the years, or Neil decreased her presence at them, and so his life remained a mystery. She had no real reason to doubt what he said, but when she had seen the relaxed chatting of the other spouses at the few events she did attend, her suspicions had flared. If this was another rule like no reading mail and no reading texts, this wasn't so much the company's rule but Neil's.

As the doors dinged behind her, Alex made a note of the fake smile on Neil's face, and nearly bumped into a woman almost running the opposite direction. She felt it, then the combination of anxiety, fear, and smug pride, the psychic picture of every other adulterer that she had ever known. It hung around her like a miasma. So, this was her then Alex's eyes flickered for just a second and catalogued the features. Dark hair, voluptuous, olive sin. "Hey there, lady," he exclaimed loudly. Too loudly. Alex couldn't remember the last time he'd shown that level of excitement to see her. Oh well, if it was a show they were putting on, Alex was game.

"Babe," she replied, wrapping her arms around his neck and kissing him full on the mouth.

"This is a surprise," he said, disentangling himself. "Not exactly a welcome one," was not said, but still Alex caught the subtext. She held up one hand, shaking the take-out bag.

"I thought we could have lunch together," she said, "I have to leave for a bit in about an hour." He scrubbed at his face, and she saw his Adam's apple bob as he swallowed.

"Saving the world, one website at a time?" he asked with a too toothy smile. His cheeks crinkled damn near all the way to his ears.

"Something like that," Alex said. She stepped closer, smirking coquettishly. "Think we could find somewhere private?" Neil's eyes darted over her shoulder, and Alex could feel fear, yellow, coming from him in waves. She could feel something else as well. Hate and love, tangled together, flowing from behind her. The mistress was there then, had to be, and Alex fought the urge to turn around. Instead she pressed closer, kissing Neil at the corner of his mouth, the spot where there was always a little bit of stubble, no matter how recently he'd shaved.

He cleared his throat. "I think we can manage that," he said, and opened the door to a small, dim conference room. As he closed it, he adjusted the drapes. With typical inappropriate timing, Alex found the words to "say my name," one of her favorite '90s songs, running through her mind in time with the beats of her heart. She lost her debit card regularly. Owed the library a small fortune in fines. But '90s lyrics, those were forever.

The lunch was superb, crispy falafel and zesty tzatziki sauce, and Alex tasted almost none of it as she struggled to keep conversation going. Neil ate quickly, trying futilely to keep his eyes off the door and devouring his gyro in three huge bites. As soon as he finished, he crumpled the waxed paper and started to get up. Alex nearly leapt into his lap, driving him into the chair. "What's the rush," she purred.

He grimaced. "I have to get back to work." Pain flashed briefly, a squeeze on her heart, as Alex realized how hard the task of seducing her husband, her own husband, was going to be. Still, over the years she had cracked tougher nuts than his. Pushing the pain aside, Alex started kissing him gently on the line leading from his neck to his shoulder, and arched her back so that her breasts pushed upward, straining at her buttons. He always was a "tit man," as he so callously called it. He responded only slightly at first, but when she straddled him in the chair, her heels falling to the carpet, and gently took his earlobe between her teeth, his shoulders finally began to relax. More importantly, other parts began to stiffen. Alex reached between her legs, undoing his belt, and with a quick motion his swollen manhood sprung from the opening. She wasted no time sliding down on it. The chair tilted slightly, and Alex began swinging her legs, taking him deeper each time. He groaned against her neck and the images began to flow. Laughter and talks of marriage with the dark-haired woman. A call made on his cell phone, talking about times and dates. This week. He planned on having her killed this week. She was grateful then that she'd followed her intuition. That she was safe in a strip club pursuing a serial killer as opposed to in her own home and in danger. Mentally, she rolled her eyes at what her life had become. Then, Alex saw an image of herself, accompanied by, and this was new, guilt. Doubt. He was having second thoughts, whether about the planned assassination or their dalliance she couldn't tell and at the end of the day it didn't matter. She had what she needed. Time. Hopefully she had bought time. He finished quickly, almost in self-defense, and she stood up, straightening her skirt.

"See you soon," she said. She was gone before he could zip up, smiling at the woman in red. "Have a wonderful day," she chirped.

*   *   *

ALEX spent the rest of the afternoon at Selah's. "I don't know," she said, over her fourth cup of tea, "I felt something different this time. Maybe if I kept it up I could, I don't know—"

"Convince him not to kill you," Selah finished.

Alex sighed deeply. "Helpful," she said.

Selah sat down next to Alex, putting her feet, clad in definitely not exotic-looking Toms, up on the scarred coffee table. "Yeah," she replied, an edge to her voice. "I'm hoping it is. Personally, I think that this is the best thing that could have happened to you." Alex looked at her quizzically. "It is. You've needed out of this marriage for a while." The blonde woman's mouth pursed as she stared into her steaming mug.

"You think so?" she asked in a small voice. Selah nodded with no hesitation.

"We all think so," she said. "The constant jokes at your expense, the rules that only seem to apply to you. And I'd be willing to bet that this isn't his first affair. You deserve better."

"Why didn't you tell me?"

Selah shrugged. For the second time in as many days, Alex heard an answer she despised. "Would you have listened?"

"Yes!" Alex exclaimed, frustrated. Selah said nothing, just gazed at her friend with calm, loving eyes. "Maybe," Still, the eyes held. "No," Alex finished, glumly. Selah gloated, shaking her fists in the air. Alex retaliated by throwing a pillow at her head, the sequins flashing in the light. "Asshole," she said.

"So, when are you going under," Selah asked, tucking the pillow behind the small of her back as she changed the subject.

Alex took another sip of tea. "Tomorrow," she replied. "Speaking of which, I should probably get going." The doorbell rang and suddenly the back room filled with the shrill tittering laughter of college girls. Selah rolled her eyes.

"Duty calls," she said. "Stay safe."

"I'll see you soon," Alex replied.

Chapter Ten

ALEX woke in her hotel room after a night filled with the kind of dreams that happen when your subconscious decides to vomit up every fear or resentment that one has. Alex's subconscious, vengeful bitch that it was, had plenty to choose from and had picked a few each from columns a through t. At least. Wearing jeans and a t-shirt, instead of her usual power suit, and her hair in a messy bun, Alex headed down to the police station. The front desk officer made a show of checking her ID with extra scrutiny before buzzing her in.

"Lookin' good," he rumbled in his deep voice.

"Thanks, Leroy," she called over her shoulder and walked straight into Hank. "Well he—"she began, but he put one finger to his lips and steered her quickly into his office. Then he closed his blinds and settled into his desk with an audible sigh of relief. "The good Captain on the warpath again?"

Hank nodded, his azure eyes huge. "You have no idea," he said.

Alex, who had known her share of power hungry bosses, winced. "And don't want to," she replied. "So whatcha got for me?" Hank handed Alex a cell phone, a hotel key (not one of the electronic cards, an actual metal key, which gave

Alex an idea of the sort of establishment in which she'd be residing), an envelope containing $200 for incidentals, and a fake I.D. Alex looked at it appraisingly. "Becket?" she asked. Hank nodded. "He outdid himself this time. Tell him I said th—" "suddenly she stopped. "Cindy Vine?" she exclaimed. "You're sending me into a strip club with an ID that says Cindy Vine?"

Hank looked blank for a moment, then "Aw hell," he said. "I'll have him change it." Alex shook her head, and tucked the ID into the envelope.

"No, it's perfect," she said, "If anyone asks I'll just say my life was predestined. Besides, most dancers have a stage name."

"You put any thought into yours?" he asked.

Alex dimpled wickedly. "Delilah," she said.

His eyes widened, "as in the woman who—"

"Took away all a guy's strength. Yup," she said, "I thought it appropriate."

Hank chuckled. "Absolutely," he replied.

"Where are my clothes?"

Hank turned an even deeper crimson and rubbed at the back of his neck. They're... not here..."He stammered.

Alex waited in vain for him to say more. He couldn't even look at her. "Okay," she asked, puzzled, "where are they?"

Hank's right leg began to shake. "At the store."

"No problem," Alex said and held out her hand, "Just give me a g-card and I'll take care of it. I'll be back by noon with receipts. And coffee if you ask me nice."

Hank began to resemble someone who was heading to their own execution. "New policy, an officer has to have the card at all times. Even with subcontractors." Alex gaped for a minute and then burst into loud guffaws. Tears bean streaming from her eyes. Just as she got herself under control she would sneak a glance at Hank's agonized face, and it would all start again. Finally, after several attempts, the gale petered out.

"Well then, Officer," she said, tucking his arm in hers, "we'd better be going."

They took Hank's vehicle, both aware of the scandal that a cruiser would cause, parked outside of a sex shop. Alex navigated, taking them through a series of rights and lefts to a nicer section on the outskirts of town. There, tucked in between a country-style restaurant and a hotel was an incongruous but inconspicuous little adult store. "Been here often?" Hank asked, when they arrived without Alex even once glancing at her GPS.

"Yes," she replied matter-of-factly. "They have a better selection than the seedier places, and I can get some club wear for when I'm there but not dancing." Hank looked in amazement at a mannequin in the window. It wore a tight blue skirt and top that tied above the waist, a sexy police officer, complete with fishnets and a riding crop. "What?" Alex asked. "Are you telling me you've never been to one of these?"

"No," he said, and when she cocked her head at him skeptically, he said it more emphatically. "No!"

"C'mon, Detective," Alex teased. "You've been single for a long time, where do you get your kicks then?"

He grinned then, shoulders relaxing and teeth flashing white. "From the internet like any sane person. "He winked, a flicker so brief that if not for the flip flop of her heart, Alex wouldn't have been sure she'd seen it, and opened the door.

Alex walked through the store, her onyx necklace firmly in place, looking at one getup then another while Hank trailed closely behind, pausing once to shudder at a life-sized fist made from rubber. "You don't have to stay with me," she said once, hanging a corset with steel rings at the neck and waistline on the rack. — too much effort to get on and off.

"Yes, I do," he said, "If I'm here with you I'm the guy with the hot chick. Otherwise, I'm just the creep wandering vaguely through the aisles."

"I can't figure out if that's sweet or hopelessly stuck in the 1950s," Alex replied.

Hank shrugged. After about 15 minutes with Alex still empty handed he blurted, "what are you looking for exactly?"

"I don't know."

"You don't know?" he asked incredulously.

"Listen," Alex said, turning to face him, "I know what I like to wear to feel sexy. But what does," she hit a provocative stance, "Delilah like to wear?" He blushed and looked around, grabbing a red combination of straps and beading in no discernible form.

"Definitely this," he said, pulling it too fast. One item not easily discernible as any particular item of clothing fell to the ground. "Damn," he said in such despair that Alex cackled.

"Maybe," she said, grabbing onto the hanger. Some outfits she liked enough to try on but discarded. Too costumy. Too difficult. Too '80s. She was hanging some rejects back on the rack when she saw it, a long gown with a low back and a neckline that plunged almost to her navel. The slits ran up to her hips. "Yessssss" she said, her voice deepening. She went into the dressing room and slid the dress down over her head.

It poured over her like milk, or wine, and hugged her around her waist. Slowly, she raised her arms and undulated. She could feel the warmth start in her stomach and begin to spread. The other outfits made her feel like a poseur. This was HOT. She bought that gown, the same one in blue, and the beaded extravaganza that Hank had unwittingly disassembled, as well as three simpler dresses, five G strings in an assortment of colors, and a pair of heels that made her ass look incredible, but still allowed her to walk without breaking an ankle.

"Now what?" Hank asked with an audible sigh of relief as he settled behind the steering wheel.

"Now we go to a box store," she answered.

"Thank God," he said.

*   *   *

AN hour later they emerged, carrying bags with pajamas, jeans, t-shirts, microwaveable meals and granola bars, an economy sized bottle of hair spray and one of those cheap palettes of make-up that cost about $5 and contained eyeshadow and lipstick in every shade of the rainbow. As they headed back to the station, they both fell silent. Alex was building her character in her mind, going through the ritual of "becoming" Sarah Jones, or Meredith Miller, or, in this case, Delilah. It was never enough to pretend to be a person or work a job, she had to believe it through and through. Delilah, she decided, had been near the top of her class in high school. Cheerleader, student council, the works. She moved out to California to become an actress, but as many people do, ended up dancing instead. By the time she came back to town to take care of her momma, she'd forgotten how and why to do anything else, her dreams had withered long before. No, that wouldn't work. She'd been watching tutorials online and a girl from vice was meeting them at the station, but there was no way Alex was going to look like a pro. Maybe Delilah was a single mom. Done wrong by a worthless ex-husband and having to strip. That would work if she was trying to get the other girls to warm up to her, but she didn't think that their perp would be into that. She tapped her finger against her chin, contemplating and reviewing the victims in her mind. All executed neatly, precisely, all left in public, hoping – or at least not caring — if they were found. Raven, the soldier, and the co— "college professor!" she yelled. Hank slammed on the brakes, spilling coffee in his lap, his eyes darting around. Alex grabbed a handful of napkins and had already started dabbing at the spill before it truly sunk in what she was doing. She cringed, hoping for a handy black hole to suddenly swallow her whole. "Sorry," she said, letting the napkins drop from her hand and becoming very interested in something outside the car window.

"What was that about?" Hank asked.

Alex stared at her lap and tried not to giggle. "Delilah is a naughty college professor," she said in a small voice. Hank pulled to the side of the road, scrubbing at his crotch with more ferocity than was truly necessary. Alex couldn't help it, she started to giggle helplessly. After a few seconds, Hank was laughing too.

"Obviously it gets a reaction," he said.

"Though not the one I'd hoped," she replied.

He looked at her, suddenly somber. "I always said you could stop traffic." Something started to build between them, powerful, inexorable as a wave. Alex looked away, pretending to rummage in her purse, before it could carry them both away. This was not the time to get lost at sea. After a moment, Hank cleared his throat and pulled back onto the street. He glanced at the clock. "Better hurry," he said, "Ortiz will be waiting to train you."

*   *   *

OFFICERA Ortiz was fit, athletic, and sexy as hell. Dressed in a sports bra, jogging shorts, and incongruent platform heels, she shook Alex's hand firmly. "Let's begin," she said. Two hours later, Alex was feeling pretty comfortable. She had already known the basics of a good strip tease, had known that it was an amazing way to get the pheromones and information flowing. She'd known for years that stroking your body made any target stand up and pay attention, imagining that her hands were theirs. What she hadn't known was that the key to moving her ass was in her knees, once Ortiz explained that, she was shimmying with ease.

"This is amazing," Alex exclaimed, her curves popping. She was also surprised at how easy it was to work the pole. "I don't know about this," she'd told Ortiz at first, "I'm pretty clumsy."

"You'll do fine," Ortiz had replied. "In fact, I think you'll like it." She'd been right. Somehow Alex found that bracing herself against the smooth silver surface made her feel safer, more grounded. She marveled at how sexy she felt, how much she enjoyed it. Ortiz seemed impressed as well. "Great job," she shouted, "rock it.". At the end of the training they clicked water bottles in a salute. "I think you're ready," Ortiz said, panting a little. "Now go get that bastard."

Alex showered at the station, the hot water pounding at the tension in her neck, the sweat of her exertion sluicing down the drains. She willed her nerves to wash away as well, the water to pound out any sign that she may give as a "tell." By the time she walked out, she was Delilah. She walked with a hip-slung prowl, her ass tick-tocking back and forth like the pendulum on a clock. Her breasts were pushed forward, her chin up. She slunk down the halls towards Hank's office, then stopped short. Hank and Captain Lobe stood in the hallway, tension palpable in the air. The Captain looked at her, one lip raised.

"Ms. Campbell, I'm so pleased to hear that you are doing something more... in line with your skillset." Hank started to protest, but Alex waved him off. Alex might mind what the Captain thought, Delilah didn't give a damn. She stretched, pushing her breasts out even farther, and stared, holding the Captain's gaze. They glared at each other for a long moment. Sergeant DuPre came wandering down the hall, a Styrofoam cup of coffee in his hand, and stopped, his eyes wide with surprise. Alex barely noticed him. She took a step closer to the Captain, not confronting, but not backing down.

"It's an honor," she said at last, her voice even, "to do whatever it takes to bring this guy down." Captain Lobe looked away first, and Alex got ready to leave.

She got into Sergeant Ortiz' car. Her bags of purchases were already loaded. She turned to Hank, who seemed to be waiting for her to say something. "I still think you should have gotten that fist," she said, expecting him to laugh. He didn't. She waited for a moment, awkwardly, then shrugged. "I'll be in touch," she said, and crouched down to climb into the sedan.

"Wait," he exclaimed. Alex sat, but left the door open, glancing quickly at the clock in the dash and calculating how long her hair and makeup would take. She looked at Hank expectantly. He ran his fingers through his hair and swallowed. Finally, "I hate this," he almost yelled.

"Hate what?"

"All of it. Sending you on this case, the deal with your husband. I just... I don't feel good about this."

Alex's face softened. "I'm not the biggest fan of my husband right now either," she replied. "As to the other, I suggested it."

Hank looked pained. "I just don't truly believe this is the best plan," he said. "I don't know — "

"Well I do," she said smiling. "Believe in me. Trust me, that strip club won't know what hit them."

Chapter Eleven

ALEX handed her fake ID to the bouncer, who examined it with little expression or interest, then grunted, unclasping the worn once-velvet rope so that she could pass through the door. It was dark inside, dark enough that it took several minutes for her eyes to adjust and be able to discern the glow from the black light on the carpet and furniture from the reflections in the myriad mirrors on every wall. By the time she had gotten her bearings, there was a woman standing in front of her. She was older, if the lines on her face and the slight thickness around her waist were any indication, and her dark, kinky hair was swept up into a chignon. She seemed kindly enough, but gave off an undeniable, no-nonsense vibe of someone who had, truly, seen it all and been impressed by none.

"You're the new girl," she said. Alex nodded. "Kurt told me to expect you. Everyone calls me Mama. Come with me." Alex followed her past the stage and through a black, concealed door to the left. The room was mostly empty. Only two other women were there, one sitting in a chair in front of a mirror and the other, wearing only a thong and a pair of boots, sitting on a couch. They both fell short when Alex and Mama walked in, appraising Alex with dark-lined eyes. "This is the locker room," Mama said. "You can have locker ten. No drugs, no men. Clean up your shit. I might be Mama but I'm not your mama. Get here before your shift. Ain't nobody wants to see some chick with a ponytail and yoga pants walking through. Right-to-work is $25 a night, due before your shift. Do you have it now?" Alex paused for a minute, wide-eyed and then started digging through her purse. It had never occurred to her that she'd have to pay to work there. She found the two lonely bills that she had tucked in there just in case, and heaved a sigh of relief.

"All I have are two twenties," she replied, "Can you break it?" The other woman sorted and dug a wad of bills an inch thick out of her cleavage.

"Small bills aren't a problem here," she said, handing her a ten and a five. "You're gonna wanna keep your money on you. We ain't responsible if anything gets stolen. Tip the DJ and the waitress or they'll make your life hell. Any questions?"

"N-no," Alex stammered. Suddenly she felt very unprepared.

"If you need me, I'll be at the bar," Mama said. "Try not to need me." And with that she was gone. The girl at the mirror muttered something under her breath to the other girl and laughed. It was not a kind laugh. Alex smiled anyway and went to her locker and shoved her small bag of clothes and her purse in it, making sure to stuff her change in the pocket of her jeans. Then she carried her make-up to an empty spot at the counter. The girl on the chair popped a bubble of chewing gum.

"What's your name," she asked.

"Delilah," Alex replied, breathing a sigh of relief that she'd remembered. She turned and smiled welcomingly. The woman did not smile back.

"I'm Destiny," the girl said, "And this is Desire. You ever done this before?" Alex briefly pondered changing her backstory, she didn't want to seem weak, but decided to stick with the story she'd come up with.

"Not like this," she replied. "Private parties, amateur nights, stuff like that." The girl sneered, and turned back to the mirror, spraying herself with glitter.

"Good luck," the girl on the couch said.

Alex started applying her make-up, contour, blush, and heavier eyeshadow than she usually used. She was working on her cut crease, trying to get both eyes to match, when the other dancers started to come in. The locker room got very hot and much louder, faster than she would have imagined. The bulk of the women paid Alex no mind, at most they gave her a look of mild curiosity. A couple gave her a brief hello. So many came and went, Alex imagined, that it was pointless to let yourself get attached the first night. What did surprise her was the total lack of pheromones, sex, whatever. She'd had her vitamins, was wearing her bracelet, and still nothing. She'd been in board rooms that were more sexually charged than this place. Which made sense, the suits and tie set lived more repressed than the rest of the world, and it had to get out somewhere. She needed to prepare herself, though, so she put her earbuds in. The familiar harmonies and lyrics kicked in and she could feel herself relax. She was so into the music, into her preparations, that she didn't pay any attention to the woman who came up behind her, didn't even notice her until she pushed Alex's shoulder. Alex pulled out her earbuds, and turned around.

"Can I help you?" she asked. Her assailant was gigantic. 5'10" perched on top of 6-inch heels. Her face flushed red, and her eyes glittered dangerously. Alex wanted to stand, conversing at thigh height wasn't really in her comfort zone, but the woman was already mad, it seemed better not to appear aggressive. Alex stayed put.

"Can you help me?" Her voice sounded like broken glass and asphalt. "Bitch wants to know if she can help me," she screeched to no one in particular. "You can help me by getting off your high horse."

"I—"Alex stammered.

"Then you can help me by getting your nasty ass outta my seat." Another woman, a young girl really, with mahogany brown eyes and brown hair, started to say something, but Alex shook her head, only narrowly avoiding rolling her eyes.

"It's fine," she said, "I'm finished." She crossed to her locker to the continued litany.

"Finished. You will be Finished. Finished working here. Finished working at any club. I know people. Fucking fancy ass new bitch." Alex let it go, this was no time for a pissing match, and shucked out of her clothes. She was sliding on her gown, it felt every bit as amazing as she remembered, when the dark girl with the big smile sat down next to her.

"Don't pay any attention to Jade," she said, "she picks a fight with someone every night."

Alex smiled back. "Welcome to the neighborhood, huh?"

"Something like that." The girl stuck out her hand. "I'm Veronica," she said.

Alex shook it. "Delilah." Veronica laughed, a charming belly laugh.

"That's my girl, fucking dudes up all day long. This your first night?" Alex nodded.

"Yeah. I used to work at a college but..."she let the sentence dangle.

"It happens," Veronica replied; "I used to go to college but... Nervous?"

"A little," Alex said honestly.

"You'll be fine," Veronica reassured, "just remember that the guys who come here all really just want one thing."

"Boobs?"

"Well, that too," Veronica laughed. "But mostly they come here to feel special. Treat those dudes like they are the greatest, most amazing, most studly thing you've ever seen, and you'll do fine."

*   *   *

"SHOWTIME!" Mama bellowed through the door, and the girls moved in unison, a mass of breasts and legs and glitter. Alex had no idea what showtime was or what she was supposed to do, but she followed the others out. The spotlights hit, and Alex's workday officially began.

"Showtime" as it turned out, was more than just the start of her shift, it meant that Alex had to parade across the stage with the other women. Some of them were obviously crowd favorites including, to Alex's surprise and dismay, the woman who had accosted her in the locker-room, Jade. Jade fell into splits at the front of her stage, her breasts bobbing, to loud cheers and caterwauls. Alex reached her turn at the front to greater applause than she had expected and flashed them her best come fuck me smile. Remembering her tutelage with Sergeant Ortiz, she turned slowly, bent low, and popped her knees, offering the crowd an apparently pleasing view of her shimmying backside. It hit her then, what she'd been looking for. The lust, the need, the wanting. Alex grabbed on to the feeling, used them to fuel her own, and strutted out of the way, making room for the next entertainer. The song ended then and the dancers dispersed, each setting out to woo a table of men eager to part with some cash for a little attention. Alex had a table in mind as well, a dark haired middle-aged man in a suit whose want she felt like a pulse. Of that other feeling, the one that was the real reason she had come, she had no sense. Not yet, anyway. She had left the stage on her way to her target when she saw the DJ beckoning to her. She remembered Mama's advice to never piss off the DJ, so she headed over with no sign of annoyance at the distraction. The DJ was any age, covered so heavily in tattoos and piercings that it was hard to tell anything else about him. He looked genuinely happy to see her.

"New girl," he exclaimed. "I'm Tony; what do you like to listen to?" Tony stood surrounded by computer screens and speakers, and so they had to yell to hear each other.

Alex though of her playlists and winced. "Nothing that would work here," she said. Tony transitioned the next song seamlessly, and the dancer on stage moved with it.

"Don't doubt the master," he said, "C'mon, who's your favorite?"

"Boy Bands," she yelled, blushing.

"Ain't no shame in that," he said. "Could be worse, you could have said country."

"Hell no," Alex laughed. "If I wanted that, I would be at Cowboy's."

"All right, blondie," he replied, "get up there." Alex waited until the other dancer had left the stage, and then climbed the stairs. She moved, unsure at first, to a heavy techno beat. Thinking back to those first few minutes on stage would cause her to cringe for years afterwards. Stiff and unsure, she moved rotely through the moves Ortiz taught her earlier, one after another. She didn't see a single pair of eyes on her; even the man she had so enthralled earlier was checking his phone. As her moves became even stiffer, her senses dulled until all she could hear or see was an ever-increasing sense of embarrassment. After about thirty seconds, though, she noticed that she knew the words to the song; it wasn't the puppet strings and mop of blonde hair that she was familiar with, but it was good enough to give her confidence. Tony had come through. The grin she flashed the DJ Booth would have gotten anyone's attention, and she grabbed the pole with both hands. She ran her hands down her body, and first one head came up, then others. She closed her eyes and pictured herself in a bedroom, teasing a dark form on the bed. By the time she left the stage, the room was alive with emotion. She took a deep breath, her normal eyes closed and her secret eye wide open She had done it.

Chapter Twelve

ALEX stumbled into her hotel room five hours later, exhausted and sore. She had a little over $300 in her purse and her head was pounding from the music and the lights. She had never been quite the combination of tired and wired as she was right then. She knew more things about more people than she ever had before. In that environment, secrets, little ones and big ones, flowed abundantly. She did not, however, have any further leads on the murderer who had brought her there.

Alex intended to sleep in the following day. She ached in places that she hadn't known existed, and no amount of water seemed to touch her dehydration headache. Others had different plans, it seemed, as her cell phone started chirping at 7am. Selah, Pasha, Hank, everyone was determined to find out how she was doing, if she was okay, what she had discovered. Even Neil got into the action, asking her when she would be back. She ignored the first barrage, but when the second wave began shortly after 9, she snapped the phone to her ear. "Undercover," she said, carefully enunciating each syllable. "It is very hard to remain undercover when my other world won't leave me alone!" The caller, who hadn't yet been given an opportunity to speak, was silent for a moment. Surprised and slightly disapprovingly silent.

"People are worried, Alex," Selah said at last. Alex dry-swallowed a couple of ibuprofen from her cache on her nightstand.

"I know," she said more softly than before. "But if I'd brought someone here to interrogate, stuff like this could ruin everything. You know this is what I do for a living."

"This isn't just about your job," Selah replied. "Have you forgotten about Neil and his plans? Because I haven't. Alex, this is serious."

"I know that!" Alex exclaimed. "Do you think I don't know that?"

"I'm not sure that you do," Selah replied. "Sometimes you act like it is serious. Other times you act like it's some sort of…"

"Misunderstanding?" Alex interrupted. "What if it is?"

"It isn't."

"But how do we know?" Alex heard Selah sucking on her tooth and knew that she had frustrated her friend.

"What I know is that you must believe this, Alex. All the way down to your bones. At least put a fraction of the effort into finding your killer that you are to finding this other one."

"Psychic discovers her husband is having an affair and has hired a hitman," Alex mocked. "It sounds like bad TV."

"Look at us, "Selah countered. "The whole group of us, we are good TV at least. Alex, listen, you need to hear this; if you don't believe it you will die. If you don't pay attention to this problem, YOUR problem, you will die."

"You sure?" Alex asked.

"I am," Selah confirmed. "You're the only one who can stop it. I'll wait for you to be in touch and I'll tell the guys to do the same. But... be in touch, okay? At least a text every day."

"I will," Alex promised. Next, Alex sent Hank a text assuring him that she was all right and that she'd let him know immediately if she discovered anything. The implication of that was, she hoped, clear. That done, she took another chug of water – would she ever rehydrate – and called Neil. He sounded chipper, more cheerful than he'd been in a while, but by the third time he asked when she'd be back, Alex's patience was wearing thin. "You seem eager," she purred, her voice barely hiding her rage. "You miss me?"

The pause was just a beat too long. "Yeah," he replied. "I thought when you got back we'd go out, Just you and me."

"And the hitman—"Alex added silently in her head. "Sure," she said before hanging up, "that would really be something."

*   *   *

BY the time she wrapped up her calls, Alex knew she'd never get back to sleep, so she went to explore the bathtub. The curtain was dingy, and a rust stain ran from faucet to drain but it was clean and deep enough, if not for luxury, then for a soak. Alex filled it with water just shy of scalding and pinned up her hair. Forty-five minutes later her muscles had finally loosened and her mind felt clearer. She opened a new razor and shaved before standing up to rinse and shampoo her hair. She touched up her nail polish and blew her hair dry, singing at the top of her lungs, and then set about making the room more her own. She shut the case files and her personal cell in the desk drawer, pulling out a condom wrapper and a Gideon's Bible. The first she threw away, the latter she set on the narrow window sill, startling a pair of pigeons cooing on the ledge. She hung her clothes on the "don't steal me" hangers, smiling again at the mess of beads and strings that Hank had found at the sex shop. She'd wear that outfit next, she thought. She moved through some yoga positions, and then spent the rest of the afternoon flipping aimlessly through the slim selection of channels, too exhausted to look at the case file and too restless to enjoy any of the shows. She spent the last hour with her earbuds in, her hands trailed slowly over her body, going through the deliberate process of intentional arousal.

*   *   *

BY the time she left for work, she was ready, in more ways than one. The same two pigeons from before were sitting in the parking lot, pecking listlessly at some gravel. Alex expected them to fly away as she got close, but they didn't, merely turned their heads this way and that, staring at her with their red-rimmed eyes. She prepared to go around them; she'd learned nothing from Vinnie if not that it was wise to never kick a pigeon, when suddenly she understood. "Tell them I'm fine. This is where I am, and I am fine," she hissed at the birds. The larger of the duo cooed twice and then they took off clumsily as

Alex glanced quickly around, making sure she hadn't been heard. She was lucky; the lot was empty. Down the street, she saw a car parked and recognized Miggs's face under his baseball cap. If the killer came into the club, she'd be ready.

But the killer didn't come into the club that night or the next. While Alex didn't learn anything about the case, her time there was undoubtedly an education. She'd learned that, despite Mama's rules, the locker room housed any number of things that would earn the holder time as personal guests of the county. Alex saw things snorted, swallowed, smoked and one horrific time in the restroom, injected. The woman looked at Alex out of half-lidded eyes. "You want some," she said, holding out the needle. Alex peed and got out. She learned how to attach her earnings to her wrist with a couple of rubber bands. She learned about revenge when Jade ended a petty rivalry by coating her body with baby oil before going onstage. The next girl didn't make it 20 seconds before she slipped and fell, snapping her ankle and cracking her pretty head on the floor. She went to the hospital. Jade laughed. Alex learned that anyone in a high and tight was easy money but that groups of businessmen were a pain in the ass – literally. Still, she couldn't help a feeling of stagnation and frustration. She could feel the time slipping away, the next murder drawing closer and closer.

On the third night, one of the dancers tapped her shoulder. "Table wants you," she said, nodding over her shoulder. Alex followed her gaze and saw Vinnie and Dave. The former was grinning. The latter just looked uncomfortable. Alex didn't flinch as she sauntered over to where a drink was already waiting. She spoke venom through a smile.

"What are you doing here?" she asked. Vinnie had started to reply when one of the dancers approached the table.

"Vinnie baby!" she squealed, settling herself comfortably on his lap. "Where you been?' He grinned his familiar wise-ass grin.

"Ah you know me, darlin'," he said, "I don't like to be tied down."

"Pity," she replied. "I'm mad at you, you ass," she said, drinking from his glass and glaring at Alex. Dave looked like he wanted to sink into the floor.

"Aw honey, you know I love ya," Vinnie replied. "There's enough of me to go around."

"So, I hear," the dancer replied, and then flounced off after planting a kiss on the top of his head. Alex quirked one eyebrow upwards.

"It's my first time here," he said unconvincingly, "he asked me to come." He jerked his thumb at Dave, who was fumbling with his phone again.

"Somehow I doubt that," Alex replied, as another girl greeted Vinnie, running her fingers across his shoulders as she walked by.

"He needed to talk to you," Vinnie clarified."

"My friends told me where you were."

"Nosy little suckers" she replied. Vinnie signaled for another drink for Alex, code that he wanted her to stay at his table, and the waitress hurried off to bring it. "What's up, Dave?" she asked.

"I found the hotel," he mumbled. "Had to go there for a delivery and it matched what you described."

"Are you sure?" she asked. Dave nodded.

"Dropped by a couple of times after that," he said. "I got pictures. If you want, I can send them to you."

Alex hugged him. "Yes! Dave, you're the best. Do you have an address as well?" Vinnie held up a dollar with a leer. Alex could see the small, cramped writing on it.

"Oh, we have it," he said.

"You're a monster," she replied, leaning over and pressing her breasts together so that he could slip the dollar down her bra

"My life is complete," Vinnie said, his eyes in rapture. Alex bopped him right where the other dancer had kissed him.

"It had better be," she said, "that's as much as you're ever going to get."

She felt it then. The tingle in her stomach, the sense of wrongness. It was thick and musky, and her stomach churned a bit. Vinnie jerked back a little, concern etched on his craggy face.

"You okay?" With a shake, Alex centered herself.

"Great, but I gotta go, it's almost my turn. Thanks so much for this." Alex mounted the stage a few minutes later, tossing a smile at Tony as she recognized the song he was playing, another hard-thumping remix of one of her favorites. He hadn't been kidding when he said he could do anything, and Alex tipped him generously for it. She grabbed the silver pole, undulating against it, already infinitely more comfortable and capable than she had been just a few days before. As she gyrated, she looked in the mirror for her target but saw nothing but flashing lights and make-up smudges. Grabbing the pole above her head she spun, facing forward, and slid slinkily down. She saw him then; the impact was like a kick in the gut.

The others felt it, or something like it, too. She could see the space around him as they moved around the room, a 2-foot invisible barrier around his table at all times. The man came up to tip her, his bill neatly folded lengthwise. The contact was too brief for any insights, whoever he was he kept his thoughts and feelings to himself, even in this sensory rich environment. The sense of him hung like a miasma though, and Alex felt that combination of fear, elations and fierce predatory instinct that she always did when she found her man. Pasha called it her velociraptor mode. "Run, motherfucker," Alex thought, "the hunt is on."

Chapter Thirteen

FOR the next few hours, Alex simply observed the man. He tipped each of the women at least once, and appeared to favor IPSs. He had a smartphone that he kept face down on the table. He was courteous enough, but he rarely smiled. Strangest of all, though, was that he never allowed a dancer to sit at his table. As the evening wore on, Alex approached Veronica about him. "What's the story on that dude?" she asked, flicking her eyes his way.

Veronica followed her gaze. "Lynx? He's a regular," she said, tugging her thigh highs up her legs.

"But he never has company."

Veronica rolled her eyes. "Yeah," she answered. "He usually doesn't let people sit down. He's a dick. Not grabbing or cheap just..."she shrugged, looking for the right word, "arrogant."

"There's a lot of arrogance here, though," Alex countered, "that usually doesn't matter." Veronica looked towards the stage; time was money and even Alex could feel it slipping away.

"I don't' know," Veronica said, "Thumper sent me over there once, thought he'd like me because I went to college. Lynx let me sit down, but kicked me out when I said I was an education major. Said he wanted a conversation, not fucking Mary Poppins. I gotta go."

Alex chewed her lip and approached the table, wracking her brain for her favorite novels from College Literature. "Playing 'The Underground Man'?" she asked. If Dostoyevsky didn't do it, nothing would. He looked up, eyes wide and an enigmatic catlike grin on his face.

"Maybe so," he said, "are you looking to be my Liza?" Alex stayed aloof, her face pleasant but neutral. He'd chew up in a second if he sensed her over-eager. Guys like him had to be in control, but didn't want it to come easily. She'd dealt with scores of them in her life.

"I'll start with a drink," she said. He kicked a chair out with his booted foot, and Alex glanced down looking at the treads. They were non-descript work boots with the bottoms worn to nearly nothing. It was his eyes that were extraordinary, a shade of gold that she'd never seen on a human before. Leonine. Alex found herself drawn to them repeatedly. Lynx, as he confirmed, didn't seem to mind. They talked for hours, broken only by Alex's trips to the stage and, when the bouncers started to glare despite the constantly refilled drinks, a trip to the closed-door couch room. She could feel him beneath her as she danced, hard against her thighs, but his hands never so much as twitched from the back of the threadbare sofa, his face never changed expression. She felt as though she could sooner romance the couch itself. Still, when they came out he tipped her generously and invited her back to the table. By the end of the night, Alex felt exhausted. Part of it was the conversation. Lynx talked quickly, rapidly enough that Alex had to lean close and concentrate to understand him, and nearly every comment seemed to be a test. He stalked her like a predator, looking for signs of weakness. Worse, though was something far less tangible. The man was an emotional black hole. In all the opinions he extrapolated on, with all the jokes that he made, he still sucked the energy out of the place. Fucking him would be like fucking an icicle. Alex took both consolation and fear from the suspicion that she would soon find out.

Chapter Fourteen

THE next morning came too soon and didn't include enough coffee. Still, refreshed and spurned by actually meeting the killer the night before, Alex woke up early and started pouring through the case files with renewed vigor. She skipped over those that she had already spent time on, wanting to start fresh. The third suspected victim was Frederick Franza, a local greenhouse and nursery owner. Frederick was 54, married, and had transplanted to The Ville from the Dakotas many years before. His daughters had graduated from one of the local high schools and, with the exception of his pop-up stand that took up parking spots outside of some of the bigger box stores in the spring and summer, was utterly unremarkable. He had a kind face, though slightly weathered from years outside. Alex looked back and forth between his file and the others she'd already seen. No connection to the college or the military. No criminal history or citations, not even a parking ticket. Member of the First Presbyterian Church for a couple of decades, but as far as Alex could tell, no other victim attended. By the time she had to start getting ready she was nearly cross-eyed and was grinding her teeth in frustration. She looked at Frederick's picture one more time. She would go into work with his face fresh in her mind. Lynx showed up earlier that night, pumping fists with

Tony on the way past the DJ stand and setting up at what was obviously his normal table. Alex played aloof again, but she could feel his eyes boring into her and when she took to the stage he was there, bill folded, and whispered to her as he slipped it into her thong. "Come see me after." She smiled and winked as she strutted to the next eager tipper. Lynx had a drink waiting and soon they were talking again. He was beyond free as ever with his opinion and had, or thought he had, facts enough to back them up. By the end of the night Alex knew more than she really cared to about where he stood on gun control – opposed, politics – far left, police brutality – convinced, science-fiction books – hated them, and on and on. He never asked Alex what she thought, not really caring unless it was an opening to tell her how he felt about things. He was equally adept at dodging questions about himself, not about what he thought, but who he was.

"Forget about Lynx," she said in exasperation, "I'm going to start calling you the Cheshire Cat." He favored her with one of his grins, then, but said no more on the topic.

While she was talking, Alex was also using her senses. She didn't get any farther there. He was sensual, that was for certain. Sex all but flowed from his pores. That, combined with Alex's special powers, kept her vibrating like a guitar string, but still she could pick up nothing. She touched his thigh once, and he shifted his leg so that her hand rose higher and she almost saw something then. Almost. But it was just a flash and blurry as if very far away. When he got up to leave, Alex sidled up to him and whispered. "Maybe tomorrow I'll leave with you," she purred. He said nothing, just turned on his booted heel and left. He didn't show up the next day, though. Alex tried to play it cool, but she checked the door enough times that Veronica came up to her, her brown eyes twinkling.

"You're breaking the first rule of dancing," she said.

"Don't piss Jade off?" Instinctively they both looked around for the woman in question. She sat in the corner, her long legs crossed, fake-laughing at a couple of truckers with outdated haircuts and bulging wallets. That was good. Unless you were a man with money to burn, Jade was best tolerated at a distance.

"No, but that's a good one," Veronica replied.

"Tell me then," said Alex.

"You never, ever get attached," Veronica replied emphatically. "Ever."

"I'm not," Alex began, then stopped. Rumors flew faster and more abundantly than pasties in that place. Perhaps it would be better for her if people believed she really was interested. Especially if word made it back to Lynx. Anything that got that cat purring couldn't be bad. Especially, as Alex had to remind herself — it never ceased to amaze her how quickly the mentality of the club slid into her head — since her end goal wasn't the same as that of her peers. She played it cool, looking down and fidgeting. "I'm just... I'm not," she finished unconvincingly.

Veronica wasn't fooled. Or, perhaps, she was. "You are," she insisted. "Everyone's talking about the two of you. I'm telling you, no good will come of it."

"I like the conversations, that's all," Alex continued. Veronica snorted, stretched so that the tattoo on her shoulder rippled. Alex had harassed her about that once, asking her if she had some Chinese characters as well.

"I'm no poseur, white girl," Veronica had said with a laugh. "100% Cherokee, so shut up, Blondie."

"Maybe, but you're not here for conversation are you?" Alex shrugged. Her tips had taken a hit the past few days, that was for certain. As long as Johns bought drinks and trips to the couch room, the house was happy, but other customers were loath to spend money on a dancer they thought was "taken." A rookie mistake, that was for certain, and Alex couldn't let anyone suspect why she was really there.

"I guess not. Thanks, V." She hugged the girl briefly, tattoo and all, and sashayed off. There were some soldiers just walking in, fresh out of boot camp by the looks of it, and they had her name written all over them.

*   *   *

ALEX should have known to be on her guard once Veronica told her that everyone was talking. She was so focused on her cover being blown that any other implications never crossed her mind. Halfway through the night, she went back to the locker room to freshen her makeup. At this rate, she would be wise to buy stock in the stuff. Alex saw the women, Jade and one of her lackeys, as soon as they entered. There was something off about them, almost predatory. Their shoulders hunched, their hands clenched at their chests. Their teeth clenched as well, bared in false smiles. Alex turned and started to rise, but she was not fast enough. Jade pushed her shoulder, hard, and Alex fell back so fast that she nearly slid off the stool.

Her martial arts training kicked in, then, instinctively, and she was back on her feet in a flash, her hands held up in a defensive stance. "What's your problem," she exclaimed.

"Bitch you're everyone's problem," Jade spat.

"Yeah," her friend echoed.

Alex rolled her eyes; she also rolled onto the balls of her feet, just in case. "I have literally done nothing to you. We've barely even spoken."

"How could you speak to anyone; you're too busy with Lynx."

"Too damn busy," echoed her shadow.

Alex had to bite back laughter. "It's my fucking job to talk to him," she answered. Jade moved closer. Alex could see her wrinkles underneath her caked-on makeup. The clumps of mascara stuck to her lashes. Her nose was long, proboscis-like, her nostrils near caverns.

"He is a regular. We have dibs on the regulars." Alex smirked. She was over this woman, had been over her. Slowly, Alex let her eyes train up and down Jade's body, let the woman feel the weight of her stare.

"How's that been working for you then," she said at last. Jade lost her mind; apoplectic didn't begin to cover it, she sprang at Alex, reaching for her hair. Alex hacked her arm away and then grabbed the woman's wrist. Jade's momentum carried her around, and soon Alex had the woman's breasts pressed on the counter, one hand behind her back. The ally, a nondescript nothing whose name Alex didn't even know, charged them and Alex floored her with a sweep-kick, taking a near-disastrous tilt on her stylish heels before regaining her balance. Jade twisted and spat, it was like hanging on to some glittered, sequined snake, and Alex switched her hold, bending her backwards. The doors slammed as Big Mama came barging in with security, and Jade immediately changed tactics.

"Help me," she whimpered, crocodile tears falling from her eyes. "This bitch is crazy."

"Can it, Jade," the older woman growled. "I saw the video." Her gimlet eyes turned to Alex. "Let go." Alex did, the adrenaline starting to ebb. Mama shook her head, her lips pursed. "Y'all know the rules; go home for tonight." Alex glanced at the clock. Lynx still had three hours to arrive.

"I didn't start it," she protested. Mama was already most of the way out of the door.

"Don't matter," she called back, "Get out." Alex muttered, slinging her makeup in her bag and climbing into her "civvies." If that witless silicone queen had lost her a day's work... but there was nothing to be done.

Alex left, catching Veronica's commiserating glance. "Tank," Alex asked the bouncer, "walk a lady to her car?"

"Don' see no lady here," he joked in his deep bass, "but I'll walk you."

"That'll do, too," she replied.

Chapter Fifteen

ALEX was still seething when she got back to her room, and grumpily punched in the order for Panda Forest, one of the only places that delivered anything other than pizza to where she was staying. She stepped into the shower and could feel the tension draining out of her shoulders with the water. Maybe it wasn't a total loss; if Lynx did come in he was sure to ask her about the fight. That could be good. Very good in fact, if he discovered that it was about him.

She was toweling off, her fuzzy pajamas in place, when there was a knock on the door. "Perfect timing," she said, and liberated the bag from the grinning delivery boy. Alex ate her noodles in bed, staring at her favorite forensic crime drama. Dinner over, she grabbed the file again, flipping through for anything she had missed. She had just pulled up a photocopy of a newspaper article "locals protest on oil expansion," when she saw it. The picture was old, a couple of years anyway, and Alex didn't recognize her without the makeup. It was the smile that revealed the woman's identity; Alex would recognize that wry grin anywhere. Veronica. She was the greenhouse owner's daughter. Her name was Christine, and she was – would have been – a senior at the University. She had two older sisters, both married and out on their own. Rheumatoid Arthritis left her mother disabled. It wasn't hard to see how she'd ended up in the club and Alex's heart hurt. Alex felt her hands and feet grow cold as all blood collected around her heart in anticipation of a fight. She had grabbed her purse, and her weapon, and was almost to the door when she stopped herself. She would do absolutely no good storming into the club. The bouncer would escort her out if she was lucky. If not, her actions would blow her cover entirely. She took a couple of breaths to calm herself and glanced at the clock. It was 1:30am. The club closed in a half-hour anyway. She spent the next thirty minutes pacing, stopping to send a text to Hank. "Need to talk in the am. In Person," it said. She half expected a reply, but none came. She hoped that he had been able to sleep. Or someone was keeping him occupied, a sick part of her brain supplied. The brief stab of jealously she felt at the thought surprised her. "Not now," she muttered. At 2:05 on the dot she pulled open her second phone, the one she took to work, and texted Veronica. "Hope the night finished okay." She waited seven agonizing moments for a response. "Was nice without her here, actually. Missed you, though. Go to sleep." Alex breathed a sigh of relief and pressed the K. She'd try. She didn't think for a second that she would succeed, but she'd try.

*   *   *

IF asked, Alex would have sworn in front of judge and jury that she had lain awake the entire night. She must have dozed at some point, however, because the ring of her phone startled her, brought her to sudden if discombobulated wakefulness, or at least semi-wakefulness. "Thanks for getting back so soon," she croaked.

"It's not that," Hank said. "We have a new victim. Possibly related. How soon can you be here?" With that, Alex was truly and painfully awake. She could feel her heart pounding in her chest.

"Oh God," she moaned, "female?"

"Yeah."

"Brunette?"

"Yes, Alex, I'm sorry, I can't go into details now," Hank replied. He sounded stressed.

Alex was crying. "Hank, quickly please, is it a young girl? Twenties?"

"No," he said, "fifties." The strength ran out of Alex's legs and she sat down on the bed. Hard. "—so, we need to hurry."

Alex missed the first half. "I missed that. Say again."

"It was by an Elementary school, we need to hurry," Hank repeated. "I'll text you the address." They hung up and Alex gathered what she would need to prepare herself. She grabbed her bracelet from the nightstand and quickly washed down her vitamins. She was going through them quickly. She would, however, have to grab some coffee, hurry or not. As tired as she was, she was having difficulty focusing, let alone being aroused. She always said sex drive and excitement were like muscles to her, they just got stronger with use, but like any muscle, it was getting overworked and tired.

Even with a stop for an extra-large latte, Alex pulled up to the crime scene twenty minutes later. She started to flash her

ID to one of the uniforms guarding the parameter, but he must have been warned of her arrival because he nodded and stepped aside to let her through before she'd gotten the plastic rectangle out of her purse. Hank was deep in conversation with some techs when she arrived, and cameras flashed. The car pressed against an electric pole, its bumper crumbled around it. In the front seat a middle-aged woman bent over the steering wheel, gruesomely suspended by her seatbelt. There was soccer accoutrement in the backseat and a litter of fast food containers. The victim must have just dropped her children off at school. Alex's heart twisted, and she took a moment to say a quick prayer for the family left behind. "Ready for me?" she asked Hank without preamble. He looked at her and nodded tersely, and Alex reached out and squeezed his forearm. Just for a second. She knew that he took cases like this personally, and with the pressure coming from the precinct this was sure to be hitting him especially hard. Alex closed her eyes, willing her senses to heighten. It was slow going, and for a few frightening minutes she thought that the last few days, weeks, had been just too much, that she had nothing left. Then, a flicker of warmth bloomed low in her belly. Alex focused on that. She rifled through her likely fantasy subjects, but none of them tickled her fancy. She opened her eyes and saw Hank, and suddenly he was there, sitting in between her legs as she rubbed the tension from his shoulders, wrapping her arms around him and sliding them down his chest. "Him again?" she thought, but by then the flicker had bloomed into a flame. Alex shifted her weight slightly, letting the seam of her pants rub slightly. There it was, the feeling of opening behind her eyes. She raised her lids then, and looked around. A sickly yellow-green aura hung around the car, the color she associated with Lynx. It coagulated in a pool ten feet from the victim's car, where the woman herself slouched in the seat. There were no traces of anything on the woman herself. No rank of fear. No sorrow. Just nothing. Impersonal, then. She may have not even known that he was there. Alex walked towards the invisible to anyone but her pool and stood in it. It was that same sense of a black hole that she felt anytime she was near the man himself. She looked at Hank and nodded. Crossing to him, carefully so as not to disturb even so much as a nugget of gravel, she looked intensely into his eyes. "We need to talk."

"At the station or away?" he asked. Alex chewed her lip, considering.

"Away would be best," she replied. He looked at his phone, computing times.

"I'll meet you at one at My Thai," he said at last.

"See ya then," Alex replied. She had planned, initially, on going back to her hotel room to get some sleep; by the time she got into her car, though, her rituals, such as they were, had done their job and her veins were buzzing. She thought about stopping by Selah's salon, but discarded that almost immediately. If the assassin knew her at all, he'd be keeping a close eye on her place. She couldn't go home, and had no reason to in any case. She ended up, perhaps inevitably, pulling out the bill that Dave had given her out of her wallet, and headed down to the Omni hotel. The Omni was new; nestled down at the waterfront amongst stuffy old buildings and newer skyscrapers. Alex walked through the revolving doors, her sense still burning. She could see it all, the twittering nervous laughter of the newlyweds on vacation in the big city, the distracted hurriedness of the businesspeople, and could all but hear a dozen orgasms in a half-dozen rooms. Alex took a seat in the bar, asked for a diet coke, and looked out over the railing into the lobby. She could picture them, so strongly she could see them. Neil with his pre-coital swagger, a bit portlier now with a pouch that too many good meals and years riding a chair had brought. His smug smile. She could see the dark-haired woman sliding the key in the door, pulling off his shirt, her eyes all yes and now. Then, suddenly, it was no longer her imagination. They were there. The woman's dress clung to her hips as she clung to Neil's arm, trilling a laugh. Neil laughed as well, a full-throated chuckle that Alex hadn't heard in a while. She could feel it all. The lust, the wanting. The love. A love bigger and brighter than he had felt for her. He had loved her, sure, but always tinged, she could see now, with disdain and restraint. This woman he adored wholeheartedly and she him. It put on, magenta and gold, swirling around, hitting Alex like a fist and she gasped, turning away. She wasn't quick enough, though, and tear-filled eyes locked with Neil's hazel ones and he stopped so quickly that his shoes squeaked on the marbled floor. Frantically, Alex grabbed her belongings and headed for the door. Neil's voice rang out, echoing against the sleek black and glass dome. She could hear his shock and anger, panic. People were staring, and the brunette's mouth hung open in a lacquered "O." Alex ignored them all, walking fast and pretending to be on the phone. Maybe he wasn't sure it was her. Maybe if she played it off. He called her name again, taking a few uncertain steps in her direction. Alex barely heard him over the screaming in her own head. "Run," it shrieked, "Just run."

She didn't run, nor did she stop until she was outside the doors, taking great, heaving gasps of the exhaust filled air. Her hands were shaking so badly that she could barely fit the key in the ignition, but on the third try she was finally successful and the engine of her little red car revved into inelegant but functional life. She squealed out of the parking garage, flawlessly navigating the maze of one-way streets that made up downtown. She keyed Selah's number, but got no answer, she must have been with a client, and Alex hung up without leaving a message. She tried Pasha as well, but got the same response. There, however, she left a message, telling him an abridged version of what had happened. Hanging up, she started the seemingly impossibly process of shoving Neil back beyond the waterproof compartments. Again. He didn't go without a struggle; that laugh kept clawing its way to the forefront again and again.

She knew she couldn't meet Hank in that state, so she took a moment that she didn't have to stop by a little used bookstore that she loved. It was a quaint little place tucked in a neighborhood that used to be run-down, but was slowly filling with shops and restaurants that catered to the trendy and upwardly mobile. She browsed the shelves, breathing in the scent of coffee and old books and listening to acoustic versions of Broadway classics piped over the speakers. She found a couple of books that she wanted, one old friend that she wanted to visit with again, and a copy of a book that she'd been wanting to read for years but hadn't had time. On impulse, she bought a book for Lynx as well, a dogeared Camus from the Classics section. Alex paid the bearded and suspendered young man at the cashier station, and got back into her car.

Chapter Sixteen

BY the time she pulled into My Thai, though, her focus had returned. Hank was waiting for her, and had drinks already on the table. He smiled, warmly if wanly, as she approached. After asking her permission, he ordered for the both of them, remembering her favorites down to the smallest detail. Alex was grateful, even this decision seemed a bit much. Soon she was sipping her soup, relishing the exotic and comforting combination of ginger and carrots against the creamy coconut. Hank stared, lost in his own world, mulling over what she assumed was the case, and Alex was happy to let him. God knew she had some mulling to do herself.

"You were different this morning," he said, once their plates had been cleared.

Alex sipped her soda. "How?"

"You didn't pay any attention to the victim," he replied. "None. It was almost like she wasn't even there."

"I didn't need to focus on her this time," Alex said simply, "there were no traces on her."

"So, you didn't find anything?" He sounded disappointed. Alex glanced around, looking for anyone who would hear. There was no one close enough, but still she leaned forward.

"Hank, I found the killer. I know who he is. He was responsible for this morning as well." Hank reeled back as if slapped, and the color drained form his face.

"Alex, why didn't you tell me?" he hissed. "Don't you know how much hell I've been catching from Captain Lobe for not solving this?" He ran his hand through his hair. "I could lose my job over this. I trusted you."

"He's just a tool," Alex replied. "Just a hired gun. If we nab him that's all we are getting. The weapon. Whoever hired him will just hire someone else, only then we will be back at square one."

Hank shook his head. "They turn. I can turn him. If we bring him in, he could point me to whoever hired him. I've done it before. This could be over!" Alex thought about that for a minute, then discarded it. Lynx thought himself to be a warrior. Noble. Smart. Some romanticized '40s mobster. He would never allow himself to be thought of as impersonal. A narc. Or worse, weak.

"He won't do it, though. I know this guy, Hank," she said. "I just need a little more time and I'm sure I can get them both for you." Hank stared out the window, the muscles in his jaw jumping.

"Alex, this is my case. My job. If we go ahead with this you need to report anything you find out to me and let me dec—"

"That's not how I work," she interrupted. "You hired me to help. I need you to trust me. This isn't the first time I've had to play the waiting game. We're a team, Hank." The right side of his upper lip jumped, speaking his retort as loudly as he would have. Alex held up her hands, in both surrender and stop. "I promise to call if I think he's going to hit again. I promise to get this done as quickly as possible. But I need you to trust me. It's me, Hank."

He rubbed his face, his hand scrubbing against stubble. "How long?" he asked. Alex considered. She could hear the water from the Koi pond burbling.

"A week at most," she said at last. Hank sighed deeply.

"All right," he agreed. "A week. I may go to hell on this, but I'm going to trust you." Alex reached over and put her hand on his arm. He stiffened, still stung, but let it lay there.

"Thank you," she said earnestly. "I'm going to need you to trust me on something else as well. What I texted you about last night." Hank looked wary. That hurt. Alex tried not to take it personally, she knew the expectations he was facing and the bureaucracies that he was fighting. She knew what was at stake. Still, it stung. Nevertheless, she continued, "I need someone put under protection," she said. He facepalmed, massaging his temples, and spun his other hand in a "go-on" motion. Alex explained what she had discovered about Veronica/Christine the night before and outlined the danger she faced.

Hank shredded his napkin. "So, I need to convince them to give up personnel and money to hide this girl, but I can't tell them why she is in danger because I can't tell them that we know who the perp is, is that about it?"

"That's why they pay you the big bucks," Alex attempted jokingly. Hank said nothing. He stared, distracted. Alex reached out for him, using whatever dregs of her senses remained. Nothing. It was like reaching for a brick wall. Alex felt tears well up in her eyes, and hid them with the pretext of checking her cell phone. Her emotions careened inside her. Compassion. She wouldn't have put herself in Hank's position for all of the money in the world. Fear. For herself, for Veronica, for whomever the next victim might be. For Hank. Anger. "I don't do this because I particularly like these jobs, you know," she said. " It certainly isn't for the money, either, I get paid less for this shit than I do any of my other jobs. You think I like spending my time in roach hotels or standing in blood splatter instead of condos on the beach?"

"Why do you do it, then?" he asked.

"Because I want to help! I want to do something that really helps people. I want to affect something more than some company's bottom line or do more than confirm for a wife what she already fucking knew. But more than that I do it..." She trailed off, afraid to say more, already a lump was rising in her throat. Hank had treated her with dignity and respect. They had become friends. Good friends. Suddenly, she couldn't take it anymore. Neil. The serial killer. Isolation. Her own possible death. It was just too much. She wrote a name, description, and address on a napkin and slid it across the table. "Here," she said around tears. "Do what you want to with it." She slid back so quickly that she almost knocked her chair over and rushed from the restaurant.

Alex, almost blinded with tears, walked to her car. She would warn Veronica herself. She didn't know how she could without endangering the case, but she would. That was number one. She had to get ahold of Pasha. He could advise her on where she could stay and for how long until they got her possible impending assassination figured out – somehow. She would call some of her contacts in other cities. A working vacation would not be amiss. So involved in her plans was she that she didn't hear Hank. Didn't register the footsteps on the sidewalk or him calling her name until he put a hand on her shoulder. Alex jumped, reaching for her sidearm.

"Woah," Hank said, blocking her hand. "Easy, Alex." She turned, suddenly furious.

"What?" she nearly yelled. "I gave you what you wanted. You have the information; I'll take care of Veronica; you don't even have to worry about helping me solve the issue with Neil – who saw me catching him in his affair today, not that you asked, so what, Hank?"

He reached out, and tucked one hair behind her ear. "What do you do it for?" he asked softly.

"You! I do it for you! I do it because you're my friend and we have each other's back," Alex melted, sobbing. He tried to pull her close and she resisted, not ready to be comforted.

"Alex, wha—" Hank began, and suddenly a very angry woman was chasing them down. A small, black leather folio was in her hand.

"You didn't pay!" Her voice was angry, high-pitched. "Hey! Excuse me, you didn't pay!"

Hank turned, exasperated. "I'll be back," he said. She was on them then, pushing the folio in Hank's face.

"This is not a bar," she said. "There is no tab. You pay!"

Hank turned away from Alex again. "You don't understand—" he began.

"No!" she replied, "you don't understand. You eat, you pay. It's that simple." With a sigh, Hank reached into his wallet and pulled out a couple of bills. He thrust them at the woman.

She was instantly mollified. "Do you want change?" she asked sweetly.

"Just take it," Hank replied. Alex tried to hold back her laughter as the woman rushed back inside as quickly as she had come. He looked at Alex, smiling a little. "Alex, I'm sorry," he said. "I should have asked about you. I should have checked on you. None of this is your fault. My red tape shouldn't be your concern. I'm stressed to the max, but I had no excuse to take it out on you." Alex looked at him intensely, not ready to let him off the hook just yet.

"So, you'll take care of Veronica?" she pushed.

Hank nodded. "Of course. I don't know how I will explain it, but we will figure something out. And Alex," he said as he turned to leave. "I'm sorry and I do trust you." She nodded, not forgiving — not yet — but acknowledging his apology. He held out his hand. "Still friends?" Alex paused for a moment, perhaps a beat or two longer than normal, before taking it. She did, though, and images flooded her. They were muted, foggy. She wasn't in the least aroused, the stimulants from earlier had left her system entirely, leaving her feeling lethargic and slow. Still they were there. The victims. Captain Lobe yelling her face bright red, her perfectly manicured nail in Hank's face. Headlines implying the department – and by extension Hank's – incompetence. And her. Hank holding her face in his hands and kissing her. A campground at night. A ship in a harbor. Him taking a bullet meant for her.

Alex cleared her throat awkwardly. "Still a team," she replied.

Chapter Seventeen

IF Alex had thought that Hank was a tough sell, it was only because she had not yet encountered Veronica. The girl shivered, terrified. She had a hundred valid reasons to be so, the loss of her father, any dancer's inherent distrust of the police, being woken up and taken to the station with little to nothing by the way of information – but she was also furious. When she saw Alex sitting in the conference room her eyes widened so that Alex could see white all the way around her irises. "You bitch," Veronica spat. "I was your friend and you drag me in here for what? Huh? For what. I didn't do anything! "Alex held her hands up in submission and tried to speak but the other girl wasn't done. "Fifty bitches in there doing a hundred kinds of drugs and you narc on me!"

"It's not what you think it is... Christine," Alex said gently. At the mention of her real name the younger girl wilted, all the fury leaving her.

"How did you know my name?" she asked in a small voice.

"I'll tell you everything," Alex said, softly, gently, "but we have to wait for someone." Veronica flinched, her dark eyes darting to the door. "He's a friend," Alex said, "I promise." By the time that Hank arrived, clutching bottles of water and closing the door behind him, Veronica had calmed somewhat. She was still nearly vibrating with tension, but she was at least willing to listen. Alex started to make the introductions.

"I know you," Veronica interrupted. Her eyes filled with tears as she looked at Hank. "You came to tell me about my dad." One tear fell, glittering from her bottom lashes.

"I did," he replied. "Do you remember what else I told you?"

Veronica picked at a ragged cuticle. "You said you wouldn't stop trying until you caught who did it."

Hank nodded. "Christine, we think we have found him. Well, Delilah did." Veronica looked at Alex and sniffed. "Cutting hair – "

"All day long." Alex finished, reaching out to clasp Christine's hand.

"I knew you weren't really one of us," Veronica said. Alex smiled, chagrined. Veronica turned back to Hank. "So, what now? Is there a line up or something? Because I wasn't there when it happened."

Hank shook his head. "Not yet," he said. "We're still getting more evidence before we make any arrests. In the meantime, though, our priority is to keep you safe."

"Safe?" Veronica was confused. "Why wouldn't I be safe?" Hank said nothing, but he glanced at Alex. Veronica followed his eyes. "He's been at the club, hasn't he?" Alex said nothing. Still, Veronica's face lit in understanding. "It's Lynx, isn't' it? "

"I can't—"Alex began. Veronica started to sob.

"He touched me!" she shrieked. "He said I had captivating eyes. Oh God — Oh God," she started to heave, and

Hank held the wastebasket while Alex rubbed her back. Ten minutes later, the storm had subsided. Veronica straightened her shoulders and took a deep breath. "What's next?" she asked.

"You go with me," 'Hank replied.

"To?"

"Somewhere safe." Veronica nodded; Alex could see steel in her eyes.

"Let's go then." Hank headed for the door and Veronica followed. Before she left, she turned back. "Promise me you'll bust his ass," she said to Alex.

Alex nodded, "I promise."

*   *   *

ALEX arrived at the hotel just in time – if she were exceptionally efficient – to shower and get ready for work. The problem was, she didn't feel exceptionally efficient. In fact, she felt barely functional. She tried to go through her preparations, the second set of fete day, and they only made her feel tired and nauseous. She practiced scenarios and what she would say and how she would act, and came up with nothing. No witty repartee, no new pole tricks. Instead of changing into her club clothes, Alex put on pajamas. To go in in this state could lead to nothing good. Lynx could lose interest in her in an instant if she proved herself a subpar intellectual sparring partner. Or, worse, she could imagine ending up in bed with him but seeing nothing. He didn't strike her as a long-term commitment sort of guy. Unless she absolutely blew his mind, an area in which she generally had both prowess and confidence – she was not likely to return. That night, she felt more like quick and easy, in that if he'd be quick, she'd be easy. Bed alone it was, then, with a quick prayer that Lynx would pick someone else for his post-murder celebration party. She was asleep before her head hit the pillow.

Chapter Eighteen

THE next night, she was ready. She sauntered into the club and winked cheekily at Jade, who judiciously ignored her, freshened her makeup, and headed to the stage. Lynx lounged, settled in by the time that Showtime was over. She headed to his table, a smile in place. He didn't smile back. Instead he glowered, his golden eyes gleaming ferally but his lips pursed, like a child. "How you doing Cheshie?" she asked, hoping her nickname would warm the chill a bit. He said nothing, but pushed out her seat with one boot, his strange form of chivalry. She could see mud caked in the treads. After three failed attempts at conversations, Alex grew annoyed. Lynx kept ordering drinks, thus keeping her hostage at his table, but wanted neither a dance nor a talk. Then it hit her; he was upset that she had been gone. Of course. It never occurred to him that she could take a night off; narcissism dictated that everything be about him. That resolved, Alex set out to fix it. She lowered her eyes, looking demurely through her lashes. "I know I'm not supposed to say this," she said, running the toe of her shoe up his inner thigh, "but I've missed you these last few nights." He snorted and rolled his Zippo between his fingers.

"I was here," he grunted. Alex bit back her first two retorts and aimed for completely contrite instead.

"I'm so sorry, Lynx. I didn't know you were expecting me and I had some business to take care of. I really have been looking forward to seeing you."

"I bought some fucking flowers," he spat.

Alex groaned inwardly. "Maybe I can see them tonight?" she flirted.

"I threw them away."

Alex leaned closer. "Well, then maybe you can show me something even better. Come on, handsome, let me make it up to you. Oh!" her eyes grew wide. "Speaking of gifts. I'll be right back." She retrieved the book that she had purchased the day before from her locker and brought it out, carefully concealing it from both the bouncer's and Mama's watchful eyes, giving customers gifts was hugely frowned upon. "I picked this up for you yesterday. Have you heard of him?" Lynx glanced at the cover and smiled briefly.

"Camus is one of my favorites," he replied, "I read it all in junior high." He pronounced the name CA-muss, not Ca-MOO, and Alex suppressed a giggle; his arrogance really was astounding. Outwardly, she looked down in affected pleased shyness.

"So, you forgive me?"

"Stop trying so fucking hard," he snarled, but she could tell he felt pleased. His nasty green aura suffused with something like happiness. Alex smirked. The next time the DJ called her to go onto stage again, Lynx stood up to leave. The deadline looming over her head like a sword of Damocles, Alex became agitated.

"Leaving so soon," she asked lightly.

Lynx nodded. "Yeah, but I'll be back to pick you up." Alex laid her hand on his arm and looked up, her eyes starry with adoration.

"You promise?" she chirped.

"I don't make promises," he said, his canines glinting, "but I'll be here.

"The bouncers can't see you or they won't let me go,"

"They'll let me," he said, and swaggered out of the club.

He wasn't wrong. Bubba's eyes widened when he opened the door and saw Lynx standing by his car, smoking, the cigarette pinched between his middle finger and his thumb, but he said nothing. Alex climbed into his vehicle, her heart pounding in her chest. The drive wasn't long, and they spent it with Lynx's squared right hand squeezing her thigh. He lived in apartments that were little more than glorified flophouses; chipping paint, buzzing lights, and hallways rife with cigarette smoke and stale alcohol. Alex's senses, wide open, saw everything. It was overwhelming, like being in a room full of people shouting at you from all sides. She focused on Lynx, sliding her hand around his waist and clutching at his cock while he unlocked the door. It jumped in her hand and he groaned gutturally, almost a growl. He didn't even turn on the lights once they were inside. Instead, his tongue was in her mouth, pushing, insistent, while one hand pulled harshly at her clothes. Alex responded in kind, biting at his lips and expertly unbuckling his belt. She'd dealt with this type before; where sex and violence were inexorably linked. One time had ended with a very sore jaw and the assailant at the hospital getting uncomfortable stitches. She hoped it wouldn't come to that this time. Lynx slid her onto his table; a third or fourth-hand misfit contraption covered in overflowing ashtrays. Half-cradling, half-pulling her head off the edge of the table, he started thrusting into her mouth, deep into her throat. Alex got a mouthful of foreskin and would have grimaced if she had been able.

"What do you hate about the job?" Selah had asked once.

"Driving convertibles," Alex had replied with a wicked grin. "I much prefer hardtops."

She felt his fingers probing at her vagina and spread her legs wider, clinging to the edges of the table, consciously moving towards orgasm. As always, her body followed her mind and she felt herself getting wetter, her hips working to ensure that he stroked the right place. She came quickly after that, and as she did she saw inside him just as he was inside her. Alex gasped in what Lynx assumed was pleasure as he spun her around, unidentifiable objects crashing from the table to the floor. Alex had a brief glimpse of a gas station bouquet, blooms down, in the wastebasket before her legs were on his shoulders and he was jackhammering away, eyes closed and mouth open. She probed deeper into his mind. Horrifying didn't seem to cover it. She walked through a throne room where his most prized possessions lay in piles. Money, twenties and hundreds, were piled against one wall, and a great cache of empty bottles and bongs lay in another. Books comprised a third. All around the room stood flat, unanimated people. They looked like cardboard cutouts, or bad paintings. Alex recognized the greenhouse owner, the teacher, the soldier. They were just the few she recognized out of what must have been hundreds, Alex saw in terror. His victims. So many. There were so many. At the far end sat Lynx himself, larger than life, his oversized muscles rippling as he sat, bored and shirtless, tossing crumbs to tiny naked humans who sniffled at his feet. He didn't pay any attention to them, instead his eyes were fixed with dead-eyed absorption at a movie screen playing, it seemed, a macabre sort of Greatest Hits. She hoped desperately that whatever morbid movie was playing, they were close to the climax because, based on the grunts and frantic pounding, Lynx was close to his. Alex heard herself moaning as if from far away. She saw herself on the screen, eyes wide as she looked at him. Then Raven, walking down the street as Lynx sat in his car, smug and staring. Stalking. A predator. She saw him showing someone a picture of Raven, dead, taken on a cell phone, and a handful of money being passed. The payor's face was out of the picture, but his hand was not. Chubby, smooth, the sleeve of a blazer and dress shirt visible above. Alex focused. It was a man's hand. On his pinkie, he wore a ring. Gold and garish with a gemstone too gaudy and ostentatious to be anything but real and etched with... something. A symbol of some sort, nothing that Alex recognized, but she stored it away for future reference. She could feel her vagina tightening in response to Lynx and she willed the movie to go faster. ...faster. "Faster, I need more!" she yelled, and Lynx was more than happy to respond. His hands left her ankles and dug deeply into her hips and she bucked wildly. She saw the housewife then, another exchange of cash.

"Got any more work?" Lynx asked.

"For you? Sure. You're the best, man." The other man's voice was high, nasal.

With one last grunt Lynx climaxed explosively, and collapsed forward. Alex's legs were still on his shoulders and she lay there, her stomach forced into rolls and her breasts pushed against her throat as he panted. "Hell yeah," he murmured. "Hell yeah."

Lynx wasn't much for pillow talk or post-coital cuddling. The furthest he was willing to go was to offer Alex a cigarette when he lit his own, and to shrug non-commitally when she politely refused. That suited Alex just fine. Perfectly, in fact. She wanted nothing more than to get back to her room and document what she had seen while it was all still fresh. She asked for directions to the bathroom and Lynx motioned wordlessly. She cleaned herself up and retuned, mentally planning how she would extricate herself without damaging his pride. She needn't have bothered.

"I don't do sleepovers," he said as soon as she reentered the room. Alex pouted a bit; putting on a show about how much she wanted to stay.

"Fine then," she said, pursing her bruised lips, "do you do drop offs?"

He shrugged. "I'll pay for your Uber," he said. "That work?" Alex nodded. "Good," Lynx replied, "I already ordered one."

"How about a goodnight kiss?" she asked. Lynx grinned and his eyes sparked in the dim light.

"For you? Absolutely."

* * *

ALEX arrived at her room at around four. She quickly sketched the ring and was outlining anything else she remembered, then carefully locked it all in the room's meager safe. Then she showered, scrubbing under the spray until all the smells of him were off her. She felt tender, bruised. She just hoped it would be worth it.

Chapter Nineteen

THE first thing Alex did the next morning was review the sketch that she had made, to see if it needed any changes or additions. She added a line or two and redrew the whole thing then started to take a picture to send to Hank. Her phone was dead, having been locked in the safe for 24 hours, so while it charged she flipped through the files again. Something about the victim from earlier in the week was tugging at her mind like a fishhook, but she had no clue what it meant or where she had seen her before. She started at the beginning of the file and flipped through them slowly, looking at all the pictures. She was only five or so pages in by the time her phone turned on; it sounded like a techno remix, a hundred beeps and notifications all rushing to be the first heard. Alex ignored them all; she took a picture of her sketch and sent it, along with a brief synopsis of what she had discovered the night before, to Hank. That done, she started going through the other notifications. Neil had called a half-dozen times as well as sending myriad texts that ran the gamut from panicked to apologetic to, finally, apoplectic. He had eventually, she surmised, discovered the bank accounts. "Screw you," she thought, and moved on. Almost all the rest were from Pasha, and they all said the same thing; call now. She did, and he answered before the first ring had finished.

"Are you all right?" he nearly barked. Fear had raised the timber of his voice, made him sound shrill. "Where are you? Have you heard?"

"Slow down," Alex replied. "I'm fine. You know I can't tell you where I am but I'm fine. Pasha, what's going on?"

He took a deep, ragged breath, steadying himself, and Alex realized that he was crying. "Selah's in the hospital." Alex was nearly out the door before she asked the next questions.

"Where? I'm on my way."

"No!" he was nearly screaming. She had never heard Pasha like this before, not when his cat had died, not when he'd caught his personal trainer and lover in the arms of another man, a wannabe actor from downtown, not even when a horde of sorority girls had wrecked his vintage mustang.

"I need you to tell me what happened. Pasha you're scaring me."

He nearly screamed. "Scaring you? You should be scared. Alex, you should be fucking terrified. He showed up last night. The hired gun your douchebag husband bought. Came in like he was a customer and asked where you were. When she wouldn't tell him—"his voice cracked.

"How bad?" Alex asked quietly, forcing words around the lump of guilt that made it hard to breathe, let alone speak. It was an eternity three seconds long before he spoke.

"She'll live. But Alex — he really worked her over. Broken jaw, shattered one of her candleholders and cut her face. They thought she had bleeding in her brain—" he swallowed, and his throat clicked. "But that seems to be under control now." Alex was sobbing.

"I have to come, Pasha. I have to."

"That's what he wants!" he was screaming, then, no almost about it, and she could hear the nurses rushing to hush him. "Don't you see, she almost died trying to keep you safe. Don't you undo it. Don't you dare." Alex's shoulders slumped.

"Did she get a description?" she asked.

"No," Pasha said. "He had a hat that he kept pulled down and a big coat."

"Are you safe?"

"I'm not leaving her side," Pasha replied. "They have an officer at the door. Dave is staying with some hacker friends. You know those cretins barely go out in the light of day, and Vinnie is… " He trailed off.

"Vinnie will be fine," Alex finished. "Pasha, what do I do?" she wailed. His breath hissed through his teeth and Alex could feel his exasperation.

"Finish this. Finish whatever is going on that is more important to you than your own fucking life—".

"Pasha people are dying," Alex wailed. "I'm not on vacation here, people are actually dying."

"And your best friend was nearly one of them—" he interrupted, "So wrap up whatever your business is, then do something to get this asshole put away. Selah couldn't talk much, Alex, but she made sure I would tell you that she didn't say anything. That's when he beat her I think. Alex, you owe her this. If you won't save yourself for you, do it for her."

"Okay," Alex said, "Okay. Keep me posted all right?"

"I will," Pasha said, "We love you, Alex."

She was crying again. "I love you too. All of you." Pasha hung up first. Alex sat for a while, the phone still held to her ear, afraid to put it down, to break whatever connection may remain.

Finally, she did. She lost whatever composure she had maintained then, sobbing into the pillow and slamming her fist on the bed. When finally she lifted her head, her eyes narrowed with hate-filled focus. She practiced some martial arts stances, sparring and jabbing with the air, until her heart slowed. She went back to the files then, examining every picture with painful, excruciating attention to detail. When she got to the protest picture again she stopped. There, in the right-hand corner, her face partially cut off. She recognized the woman from somewhere. Quickly she picked up her phone and did a quick search of the woman from just days before. The victim. The housewife. Her hair was different in the photo and she was wearing makeup, but that was her. The girl with her back to the camera, holding a placard, that could be Raven. Hard to tell; the person was wearing a knit cap and baggy cargo pants, but it could be. And in the back, a flash of BDUs. Pixelated black and white didn't highlight it well, but she was certain that's what it was. Her eyes scanned the caption. "A group of concerned citizens protesting local businessman," was all that it said. No mention of the business or the protest, just a blurb stuck in between Community News and the editorials and chili cook offs. "Damn it," she said, shoving the desk so hard that it banged off the wall, the shoddy drawer sliding forward and hitting her in the stomach. She pushed herself to her feet so fast that the rickety chair fell over, one of the cross supports coming loose. She left it sitting there, grabbing her phone and flinging herself down on the bed. She glanced at the clock. Two hours until she had to leave. It might be enough time. It would have to be. There was no way in hell she was missing work. "I'm nailing you in more ways than one, asshole," she muttered.

Her fingers flew from one number to another, spelling the words so badly that even autocorrect couldn't help her. She took a deep breath and tried again. The second time she had better results, if only marginally. The search results were dismal, whatever was going on it hadn't made the local news. Yet the crowd size in the photo had looked significant. Either whomever was in charge of the paper had been paid, probably handsomely, to play down the community outcry, or the numbers weren't large enough to warrant attention. Alex suspected the former. "Typical," she snarled. Her leg jiggled, and her fingers tapped the back of her phone as she contemplated. After a moment, she logged into Twitter. It had been so long that she had forgotten her password. She tried them all, including "letmeintomyfuckingaccount" before giving up and requesting a new password. It took three seconds for the email to appear in her inbox and by that time Alex was pacing in impatience. She clicked the link and logged in, using a password so profanity laced that she could hear her mother gasping in scandal from the grave. After a few searches she found it. Her eyes widened. "Gotcha, you bastard," she muttered. Alex sent an email and started getting ready.

*   *   *

SHE spent 45 minutes moving from one yoga position to another, focusing on a mental image of a flame. A former yogi had once taught her this exercise, any intruding thought would make the flame flicker as if in a draft. Alex was to focus until the golden glow stayed straight and tall for the first fifteen minutes, all she could see was a burned and blackened wick with smoke blowing in the maelstrom. Eventually, the candle lit, then flickered, and finally was still. When she had held it such for ten minutes, she got up.

Alex walked with a loose-limbed prowl, her eyes wide but her pupils narrowed. She put on her bracelet and took her vitamins, seeing every detail of the dingy room. She noticed the nicotine stains near the ceiling, the stain on the wall by the clanking radiator. With her third eye, however, she was reviewing Lynx's throne room. She was going to have to find, or make, a way to control the video. Mentally she walked up to the screen repeatedly, looking for any sign of buttons or a remote. There were none. No matter. She could make some if it came to that.

Chapter Twenty

ALEX paid more attention to her makeup, and applied it heavier than ever before. She had read an article once about war paint from various tribes of people from the Pictish of Europe that became the Native Americans. The article had talked about the psychological benefits and, as she added another layer of black to her cut crease, Alex couldn't help but agree. She applied fake lashes and outlined her lip in a deep crimson. She strode across the parking lot, noting the pigeons cooing and bobbing. "Tell him I'm fine," she said to them., "but you might want to keep an eye on things." She reached into her bag and pulled out a half-eaten granola bar from the night before and threw it too them, a little insurance would never hurt and the term "bird-brain" existed for a reason.

*　　　*　　　*

THAT night, Alex danced like a dervish. Fierce and fearless. She grabbed the pole and kicked off, spinning so fast that she could feel the metal heat up on her thigh. She stared deep into the eyes of all the men, Lynx especially, daring them, demanding that they want her all at the same time. She finally, finally finished the backbend she'd been working on, her knees spread, and her breasts pointed at the ceiling, much to the vocal and monetary approval of the crowd. Lynx thought that it was all for him of course, and, even if for all the wrong reasons, he was absolutely right. She didn't get to sit with him much. The Johns were eager to take her up on her unspoken invitation and they took Alex to the couch room or called her to tables more than ever before; much to Jade's dismay. Still, she knew enough to make sure that Lynx didn't feel forgotten, running her fingers at his nape, and watching the goosebumps rise on his flesh, winking at him from the stage. Sending him heart wrenching glances of longing as the customers led her away. She even paid Mama a tip to have his favorite IPA sent to his table. As such, she wasn't at all surprised to find him smoking and arrogant, when finally, she walked out of the door.

"Was that for me?" he asked, groping unabashedly at her ass.

"It's been for you for a while" she replied. "Now I've just been properly inspired." He kissed her fiercely, plunging his hand in her hair. By the time they broke apart, she was panting, gasping for air. "Take me home," she said.

*   *   *

HE started with no more preamble than he had the night before, picking her up as soon as they got through the door. She wrapped her legs around his waist as he pulled the top of her dress down. She had the briefest moment to hear threads snapping before his mouth was on her, teeth pulling at her already taut nipples. She had to fight the urge to start riffling through his brain right away. She was eager, so eager, but she wasn't willing to begin until she was fully "awake" and he was completely distracted. And so, she clutched at his head, running her palm over his closely-shorn stubble and rocking back and forth. She could feel the coolness of his belt buckle rubbing deliciously against her clit, and she moaned deeply in desire. Lynx finished with one nipple and let it pop, red with the pressure of his teeth, out of his mouth, and started on the other. Alex rocked faster still, her wetness soaking her panties. With a guttural, deepthroated noise, Lynx reached for his waist with one hand. Alex heard the sound of a zipper and then he was inside her, his dick shoving past her underpants. Three steps later they were on the couch and he was deeper still. Alex came deliberately, explosively, her eyes focused on him, but not seeing him. Instead she saw the movie screen, ran up to it and plunged her hand inside. It felt like gelatin or algae. Sickening and thick. The scene shorted a bit and Lynx flinched. She bit his shoulder, squeezing his organ with hers and he resumed. Inside his temple, Alex concentrated. "Who is he," she muttered, "Who hired you?" For a moment there was nothing and then he was there, fuzzy at first with the same flat, non-entity look as all other humans in his room. Then, a face. Narrow, beaky nose. 10-dollar haircut above a 2000-dollar suit. Alex memorized his face, burning it into her mind. A phone was next, numbers and dates. She memorized those as well. Somewhere, Lynx was coming, Alex closed her eyes and then she was back in her body and with him. "Mmm," she murmured, "You're incredible." He seemed distracted and fell out of her, walking to the bathroom with his pants still around his knees, without saying a word. Alex's mind raced. What she had done, looking for a specific vision, messing with his mind, was risky. Passive observation was rarely noticed, but when deliberate action was taken people could tell. She eyed the exit, then the bathroom door. She could maybe make it outside before he caught her, but then what? She chewed her lip and planned her next step. There was an ashtray she could use as a weapon if necessary. Heavy, irregular, with edges she could grip. The toilet flushed, and Alex shifted forward on the couch, ready to spring. Lynx turned, not angry, which was good, but obviously confused. He sat next to her and pulled open a zip lock bag from the coffee table. He picked the green leaves and packed them into a glass bowl, taking a deep drag with his Adam's apple bobbing up and down as he tried not to cough.

"Want a hit?" he croaked. Alex shook her head. "Don't be a fucking prude." He held the bowl out again. Alex drew deeply enough to make the leaves glow orange, but shallow enough so that she took only a wisp of the acrid smoke into her lungs. A wisp was enough; college had been a long time before, but it seemed to pacify Lynx. He relaxed as he took one hit after another, his shoulders lowering and his eyes turning red rimmed. Alex moved behind him, feeling the worn and grainy top of the couch against her ass, her back pressed against the paneling. Slowly, she kneaded the thick cords of muscle running from his neck to his shoulders, working at them until they finally began to loosen. While she massaged, she recalled the text messages that she had seen. Lynx's next meeting with whomever had hired him was on the 18th. She counted days and then groaned inwardly. She leaned forward, her breath hot against his ear.

"I thought," she said, "that maybe tomorrow we could go on a date. See what you look like in the light." He leaned aback and pulled her arms around him and laid them on his chest.

"You're not getting sentimental on me, are you?" He was interested, she could feel that, but hesitant too.

"You're the one that bought flowers," she said, her tongue flicking out against his ear. She could feel his cheeks move as he smiled.

"Can't," he said. "I have an appointment." He was wavering, and she pressed on.

" Take me with you," she wheedled, "I'll be VERY impressive." He was quiet for a moment, considering, and her heart sank. Then he sighed, sinking farther into the V between her legs.

"All right," he said, "Meet me here at 6. You'll miss work." Alex leaned awkwardly around him and kissed him.

"You're worth it," she whispered. "Should I call a ride?" He turned around and slid her underwear, stretched beyond all usefulness, down off her feet.

"In a little while."

Chapter Twenty-One

ALEX was at the station at 8:00am the next morning. She had showered, and was wearing a pair of slacks and feeling more herself than she had in a while. The precinct was surprisingly quiet, that lull between the craziness of night and the hustle and bustle of less dramatic complaints during the day. Once the officer buzzed her through she fell into the cacophony of the start of the shift. Several people called out hellos, and Alex waved, smiling over her shoulder, but didn't slow down, clutching her coffee in one hand and her phone in the other. Sergeant DuPre appeared, seemingly out of nowhere, right in front of her. His smile flashed white under his cop-stache. Alex stutter stepped around him, a splash of her coffee falling to the floor.

"Busy day?" he asked nasally.

Alex flashed a smile at him too. Brief, perfunctory. "Hope so," she said, and stepped into Hank's office. He swept her into a hug, squeezing her tighter than he had ever before. "What's all this—"she said with a laugh that cut itself short when they broke apart. Hank's eyes were bright with tears.

"I heard about your friend," he said. "I went and saw her. Alex, it's bad. I've been so worried." He shook his head, fending off the protest he expected. "I know how strong you are, Alex, how smart, but I've been sitting here not able to help," he gestured to the pictures on his wall, "Not able to help you, not able to help them and after I upset you last time," he swallowed, his throat moving up and down, "I couldn't lose you. But you did it. You're safe and you did it."

"Not yet," Alex replied, "but we will." They spent the next hour pouring over the items on his desk, their heads close. Alex was aware of the smell of his aftershave, the heat from his body, but it was distant, far away. Most of her focus was on the sketch that she had sent to Hank. Next to it was a printout of Hartmann Enterprises, the company that owned the oil pipeline whose progress had been halted, stalled at the river by an ever-increasing public outcry. The images matched perfectly. Next to them was a glossy 8X10 of Nathan Hartmann. His wiry hair was greasy, slicked back, but the thin lips and smug grin, his moist skin that airbrushing couldn't completely erase, those were the same that she'd seen inside Lynx's head.

"You're sure?" Hank asked. She nodded, her eyes feral.

"Yes," she said. Her voice was low and angry. "I'm sure; let's go through it again."

*   *   *

PLACING the wire was difficult, but Alex took a minute to give silent thanks that Lynx had agreed to a date, there was no way that she'd be able to hide that black box, small as it was, at the club or worse, at Lynx's hovel. After rejecting several placements, Lynx favored his hands on her waist and thighs, they settled in taping the device under Alex's full breasts. She put on her dress, smoothing it over her curves and examining herself from every angle. The dress was incredible. White and black and stretchy with a high neck that did absolutely nothing to detract from the lines of her body. It poured over her skin like milk. It was nothing that she would wear in her civilian life. Alex absolutely loved it. "I think that's good," she said to herself. Finally, she fastened her onyx necklace around her neck. That part of her work was over, all her senses would need to be completely focused on the task at hand, specifically nailing the asses of Lynx and Nathan Hartmann.

She slinked back to Hank's office, once again narrowly avoiding Sergeant DuPre, who was coming from the Cafeteria. "Jesus, DuPre," she exclaimed, not quite joking, "don't you ever work?" He guffawed, a jack-ass's idiotic bray, and Alex felt a small fissure of something from him. There was not time to look deeper into it though, and whatever closed-door liaisons may or may not be happening didn't affect or interest her in any case. She closed Hank's door behind her. "How do I look?" she asked, posing so that Hank could look for tell-tale signs of the wire. His eyes widened slightly, and his cheeks suffused with red.

"Incredible," he replied. Alex's eyes crinkled.

"Thank you, but how do I LOOK?" He startled then, and the red deepened to crimson. He came close, running his hands over the fabric of her dress and walking in a slow circle around her. He reached her front and stared, a long, searching look. Alex found herself pulled into his eyes, the dark lashes so long that they tangled in themselves. Slowly, his hand trailing from her waist, he stroked her cheek.

"Incredible," he whispered again. They moved closer and her hand slipped up his chest to rest on his shoulder. The quick rapping of a hand on the door broke them apart. Sergeant Ortiz joined them, accompanied by someone Alex didn't recognize. The newcomer was tall, over 6ft with a shaved and gleaming face. His shoulders nearly filled the door and his face was simultaneously blank but intense. "Everything in place?" Hank asked him.

"Affirmative," the officer replied.

"Is this Miss Campbell?"

" Yes," Hank replied. "Please make sure pick up is arranged for her after."

"Roger that," the man agreed. "My boys and I will be watching." He turned on one shiny boot and left.

Sergeant Ortiz looked at Alex. "Are you sure you're ready?"

Alex took a deep breath. "Ready," she said.

Chapter Twenty-Two

LYNX was late, and for a heart-stopping 15 minutes Alex found herself standing outside his door, alternating between knocking on the flimsy particleboard door and leaning against the chipped paint on the cinderblock walls. Twice she almost called Hank to wave off the whole thing, but each time she held back. "Just a few more minutes," she thought to herself. "Just a few more." She drew the attention, unwilling and unwanted, from the other residents and by the time Lynx arrived, completely without apology or explanation, Alex had turned down offers for three parties, two drug deals and a threesome. He hadn't bothered to dress for their date, was wearing a faded heavy metal t-shirt over a long sleeved thermal, and tattered jeans. His color was high, his cheeks pink and his eyes glassy.

"You're fucking hot," he said by way of greeting. She simpered, lowering her eyes and smiling slyly. They walked arm in arm to his car, and Alex got in, clenching and unclenching her hands to steady her nerves.

By the time they arrived at the restaurant she was calm. It was a kitschy chain restaurant, the wall decorations ordered in bulk from some mail-order program specializing in Urban Country. Someone was blasting on the loudspeakers, warbling on about booze and women and heartbreak. Lynx led her past the hostess station, through the maze of wooden tables and peanut shells, past the bar and to a high-sided booth where someone already sat, a half-eaten bucket of rolls in front of him and a petulant look on his face. He saw Alex and the look deepened. A deep crease, what Alex's grandmother had always called an "I want" line, appeared between his brows and the creases above his jowls deepened. "I didn't know we'd have a guest," she whined. Lynx grunted and slid into the booth, nodding at the waitress to bring her over. He ordered without looking at the menu, a ten-ounce steak, extra rare, baked potato with butter and sour cream and a house salad with ranch. He ordered the same for Alex without asking and pulled out his phone. The silence spun out, awkward and oppressive. The waitress brought the food and Lynx tore into his, sawing off huge chunks of steak and shoving them in his mouth. Alex had no idea what kind of pissing match she had stumbled into, but she felt that she, or at least her presence, was partially responsible. She thought of the van, parked somewhere nearby, stuffed with people who were depending on her to bring this case home, and looked at Nathan with feigned interest. "So," she chirped, "How do you two know each other?" Nathan cleared his throat, his beady eyes moving down to Alex, to Lynx and back again.

"He subcontracts for me sometimes," he said at last.

"You must be a man of good taste," she simpered. She turned to Lynx, "You never told me what you do," she said.

He slid one hand up her thigh and squeezed just a little too hard to be romantic. "Construction," he said, briefly.

"Well," she said, looking at the men conspiratorially, "I do know him to be good with his hands." One thin lip rose in disgust and Lynx squeezed her thigh again, his pinky finger sliding like a whisper between her thighs.

The conversation petered out after that. She'd thought that, Nathan having already pegged her as a brainless slut, she ought to play off that, but she realized too late it was the wrong tactic. It made her, to a man like that, easy to dismiss. Alex took a deep breath and tried again. She looked at Nathan, her brow furrowed.

"Do I know you from somewhere?" she asked. "You look familiar." He took his time chewing, reaching down to adjust his coat with greasy fingers, and looked at her with shrewd, piggy eyes that crawled over her body.

"I doubt it," he replied. "I travel extensively and when I'm here my office is downtown." The implications of this hit Alex like a brick to her chest, and she had to fight the rage that came over her. A hand jab right under his second chin would do wonders for his arrogance. She thought about pushing, telling him that she'd seen him on the news, but knew instinctively that it would be too far. Instead she focused on her meal. Her dining companions' plates were clean, so she put her head down and willed herself through her steak. Her preference was medium rare, and the blood seeping from the meat was making her ill. It didn't taste too bad, actually, as long as she didn't look.

Once the waitress cleared the plates, Nathan slid a manila folder across the table. "I have a new project," he said, "If you're interested."

Lynx nodded. "You know I am. Never got paid for the last one, though." The businessman waved his hand at the folder, the light flashing off his ring. Alex nearly choked on the chewy meat. The large, vulgar black stone swallowed light, except for the filigreed symbol in the center. That gleamed like a beacon.

"It's in there. I assume you'll call with any questions?" Lynx nodded as the waitress came with the check and Lynx stared pointedly at it until Nathan sighed and reached into the breast pocket of his blazer. Lynx smirked at Alex, obviously pleased that he had gotten their "date" funded by someone else. "Cheap bastard," Alex thought. They rose to their feet and instantly Alex's heart hammered in her throat. She had what she needed, it was time.

Alex kept her head down as they exited, Lynx's hand at her waist. With the folder handed over and Alex's complete lack of interest in it, both men seemed more at ease. Lynx was happy, even the corners of his Cheshire cat's mouth pulled into a self-satisfied grin. Once the wooden door had closed behind them, Nathan turned back and extended his hand, "I appreciate it, man," he whined.

"No problem," Lynx said, and clasped the white soft hand with his veined and calloused one. And then all hell broke loose.

Chapter Twenty-Three

"FREEZE!" The large officer from earlier in the day materialized suddenly, rising from behind a minivan in the front row of the parking lot. Nathan did as the officer commanded, though not out of any sense of obedience. Instead, he seemed to turn to stone, the only signs of life were the blood that suffused his cheeks and the fierce pounding of the vein in his forehead. Then he stepped to the right, trying to distance himself from Lynx and Alex. That was not the right move. The short officer jerked his head slightly, never taking his weapon or his eyes off the trio in front of him, and in an instant a swarm of body armor and weapons surrounded Nathan. He hit the ground with an audible crack and started shrieking, unintelligible sounds proclaiming his innocence and threatening lawyers and who knows what else. One of the men grabbed Alex as well, and she jerked away with a caw of indignation.

"You bastards!" she yelled, "get your hands off me!"

"Sorry," the officer muttered as he flung her face down, pushing her nose into the asphalt. She made sure that she bumped into Lynx on the way, snatching the folder from him and pinning it under her body. Alex could taste dirt and oil and she bucked, wailing as her hands twisted behind her back. With a practiced single snap, the cuffs were on her wrist, loosely, but good enough for show. Lynx, ever the survivor, had taken advantage of the chaos to run. He was surprisingly fast, his heavy boots clumping on the sidewalk, his eyes wild. He swung at the first officer who approached him, and his fist connected with an audible pop. Blood poured down the officer's face, a gory crimson half-mask. Lynx ducked under the arm of another officer, swinging with his heavily muscled leg, and the uniform staggered. The cop with the broken nose reached for his belt and pulled a weapon. He steadied it with both hands and pulled the trigger.

"No!" Alex shrieked, thinking of the information, evidence that could be lost, but hoping she sounded like a desperate lover. Instead of the flat boom of a bullet, two wires exploded from the barrel. They struck Lynx's torso and suddenly he was writhing, guttural grunts, almost orgasmic, coming from between the gritted teeth. He didn't stop fighting, though, didn't stop trying to get away. The officer pulled the trigger again, holding it this time, and Lynx was down, his back arched and his legs kicking wildly. As soon as the current had stopped the cops wasted no time, three of them were on him, subduing him with no little effort. Then, just as suddenly as it had begun, it was over. Officers shoved Nathan and Lynx unceremoniously into vehicles. Boots approached from behind Alex and gentle hands helped her to her feet. Hank searched her face briefly, his mouth set in a hard line but his eyes soft with concern. She nodded, almost imperceptibly and flicked her eyes to the folder, scuffed but intact, at her feet. Hank picked it up.

"See you soon," he said, and handed her over to Sergeant DuPre. Alex had not seen him during the confrontation, but that hardly surprised her. Not as much as seeing him now did. Her breasts hurt where the box from the wire had been ground into them. She wished that she'd had time to turn it off; she knew that once the adrenaline wore off she was likely to cry. Tears of release if nothing else.

"Good to see you working for a change, Sergeant," she teased Dupre. He said nothing, just loaded her into his unmarked vehicle.

As Alex slid across the worn backseat of the crown Vic, the handcuffs caught on the seatbelt. "Can we do something about these," she asked, rattling the chain slightly.

"We'd better not," he clipped. "Need to keep up appearances." His voice was short, brisk, and Alex almost wished for his idiotic smile. He closed the door with a metallic thunk and climbed in front of her, tossing her purse carelessly on the seat beside him. As they eased out of the parking lot, Alex felt the adrenaline flow out of her and she slid down the seat, her face turned gratefully towards the air blowing in through the cracked window. She kept waiting to feel elation, the almost arrogant rush of a job well done. It never came. Instead she just felt exhausted, gnawed upon by an inexplicable lump of dread in her stomach. DuPre cursed as two pigeons swooped, almost hitting the windshield. Halfway done. Everything that Alex had done and everything that she had been through and she was still only halfway done. There was still another killer out there somewhere, one with whom the stakes were even higher. She thought of Selah, still unable to leave the hospital and Pasha, who was too afraid to. They passed the first turn off to the precinct, and then another. Alex thought little of it; downtown was notorious for ridiculous construction and even worse drivers; they didn't call that area spaghetti junction for nothing. When they passed the third turn, however, she began to grow uneasy. Uncomfortable. The position of her hand pushed her ribcage forward and the tape on the wire was pulling slowly yet painfully from her skin.

"Hey DuPre," she said, her voice lighter than she felt. 'You missed a couple of turns back there." He didn't answer, his eyes didn't even flinch to the rearview mirror as he weaved in and out of traffic. As the street numbers got higher and the houses more dilapidated, Alex felt her heart sink. She spoke again, hoping someone – anyone – was listening. "26th avenue... Where are we going?"

"Shut up, bitch," DuPre growled. It was a voice she had never heard before. Gone was the foolish laughter, the shit-eating grin, this voice was flat, cold. He reached up to rub the back of his neck, and as the collar slid, she saw the scratches. Three or four of them. They started at his hairline and reached downwards. They were wide but shallow. Fingernails. Alex felt the jittery rush of adrenaline. Her mind was not panicked. Moving fast enough that the world seemed to roll by in slow motion. She could read every tag from every graffiti artist, smell the grease of the fast food joints.

"I knew I never liked you, DuPre," she taunted. He did not reply.

They turned a corner where red and blue lights cut through the approaching dusk. Traffic eased slowly around the obstruction. DuPre cursed under her breath, pulling down the sun visor and sinking low in the seat.

"Afraid of a few cops?" Alex said, thinking of the wire and especially of Hank who, with any luck, was already on his way.

"One word," DuPre said. "One sign and I'll make it hurt. Maybe give you a chance to read my mind before you die." He drew parallel with the officers, his head facing forward but she could see his eyes focused on the uniforms. Deliberately, Alex pushed her head and shoulders against the back of the seat, sliding her wrists under her ass so they rested under her thighs. They had just passed the first vehicle when the phone rang. DuPre picked it up. "What?" he barked tersely. On the other end of the line, someone was speaking rapidly. Alex slid closer to the door, out of the line of sight of the rearview mirror and eased first one foot and then another through the loop of her arms, silently thanking her yogi. If she got out of this, the instructor would be getting one hell of a gift basket. "I have her," he said, "I'll call when it's over." Alex reached up to her left ear, sliding the delicate wire from her lobs. "Your husband sends his regards," he said. Four blocks ahead, Alex could see brake lights disappearing under a train trestle. She would have to be fast.

"I can't figure out who's the biggest coward," she growled. With one hand, she carefully inserted the earring into the keyhole on the left cuff, searching for the button that would release her. "Him for sending you to take out a woman or you for getting your ass kicked by one." She felt the wire slide further into it, seeking the sweet spot. Two blocks. She hoped he would yell, blocking the telltale sound of the click. Nothing. She eyed her purse. Her weapon was inside, and she had the feeling she would need it in the near future. It was too far away;

beyond the center console and within reach of the villain himself. She had no choice but to do without. "I hear you took to her with a bat and a candlestick; I have to think you are compensating for something."

"I said SHUT UP!" the assassin roared. That was it.

Chapter Twenty-Four

WITH a jab and a twist, Alex freed one hand just as DuPre began to step on the breaks. He looked into the rearview mirror and his eyes widened. Without pausing to think, or doubt, Alex pulled the handle and dove from the car, protecting her head with her hands and rolling as she slammed into the pavement. The back edge of the door frame slammed into her ankle and dragged her for a few feet before she was able to jerk free. She felt the warm rush of exhaust as a pickup truck missed her head by inches. Alex jumped to her feet, ignoring the stabbing pain in her ankle and the blood running from her elbow, ignoring the squeal as DuPre slammed on the brakes, ignoring everything, in fact, but a desperate drive for survival. She sprinted out of the road, heading for the steep incline to the train track. One heel caught in the gravel and tore off and Alex, hop-stepping, shucked off the other. The gravel tore at the soles of her feet, but she drove on harder than before, her eyes fixed on the ridgeline. She heard DuPre yelling, and saw a puff of dirt explode to her right in the split second before she heard the sound of the shot. She started running in a zig zag pattern then, going more and more slowly as the incline grew steeper.

She still could not see the top of the hill. Behind her, the thudding of footsteps and the crunching of the dry grass alerted her to DuPre. Longer legged and unwounded, he was gaining. The long, sonorous double blast of a train horn split the air. Alex glanced to the left and saw, to her horror, the gray and yellow engine of a freight train cutting into her path. Soon her zig zags wouldn't matter. Suddenly, the air filled with gray-white wings. Pigeons, dozens of them, poured in a cyclone from under the trestle. They descended upon DuPre in a fury, picking at his eyes and coating him in foul white splotches. Vinnie followed shortly after, a blur of ripped denim and profanity who appeared seemingly out of nowhere. He rushed without preamble into DuPre, shoulder checking the thinner man. Vinnie's filthy skycap fell off of his head, and DuPre's next shot went wild. Alex burst forward with a last push of speed. Behind her, she heard the sharp thud of impact and Vinnie's brief cry of pain, but there was no time to investigate. She dove across the tracks with mere yards to spare. The horn pounded into her head like a hammer as she tumbled, seemingly endlessly, down the other side. When gravity and momentum finally released their hold, Alex lay in a panting heap, unable to get up. The sky spun above her head and something hot and sticky coated one side of her face, sending fresh spurts of blood with every heartbeat. Her ankle joined the symphony of pain with deep throbs.

"Let him be okay," she whispered repeatedly. "Please, let him be okay." Still, the train cars trudged by, creating a blessed barrier between Alex and her assailant. She struggled to her feet, falling once before standing, and testing her weight gingerly. The ankle held her, but barely. She couldn't go far. She wanted to go back to Vinnie, to check on him, but she couldn't do that, either. Her breasts heaving, Alex scanned the area. A hundred yards away was a sickly yellow cinderblock building. One wall was piled high with debris. Old tires, dumpsters, and metal sheeting fought for territory with split bags of trash. Alex took off at a halfhearted, shaking jog. As the last of the train cars passed, she hid, tucking herself into the dark triangle between a sheet of aluminum and the dilapidated wall. She focused on slowing her breathing, cringing at the echoing whoosh all around her. She heard gravel crunching, the steps slowing as DuPre approached. Alex pressed her face tightly against the wall, peering through a miniscule crack, her back feeling very exposed. The sound of boots drew closer and then he came into sight, walking away. He traversed the length of the building down to the end, kicking over tire piles. He turned and headed back her way, and Alex drew back from the crack, tucking herself lower and straining for a sound, any sound.

Timing would be everything. If hers was off, even a little bit, she was dead. Her blood pounded in her ears and she rolled onto the balls of her feet, wincing at the pain in her ankle. Closer, closer. It was time. Alex sprang forward, pushing off the wall and shoving the metal sheeting ahead of her. She landed with a crash, feeling the mass of DuPre underneath her. She bounced a few times, grinding her knees into the metal and the man underneath it, and DuPre let out a chuff of pain. She scrambled up quickly, grabbing the metal and flipping it. A hot line sliced across her palm, but she ignored it, diving back towards the ground where DuPre was pulling his weapon. She grabbed the side of his gun with one hand, rolled the other into a fist and punched him three times rapidly in the face. His nose cracked and crimson stained his pathetic excuse of a moustache. With a sinuous slithering movement, she rotated, wrapping her legs around DuPre's shoulder and pulling his wrist near her ear. All her instincts were shrieking as she saw the sleek blackness of the gun drawing closer, but she shoved them down and pulled harder still, yanking until she heard a snap and DuPre screamed. His arm went limp and he dropped the gun. Alex swept it out of reach, grabbing a concrete parking barrier and allowing inertia to carry her around. Ortiz would be proud. DuPre twisted then. He broke her grip and brought his hand around in a chop to her throat. She turned her head, and he connected with her ear instead. Alex was instantly dizzy... she tried to sweepkick him, to knock his feet out from under him, but she made the mistake of putting her weight on her bad leg. Her ankle gave way and she fell to the ground. DuPre charged for his weapon. She grabbed his feet as he ran by, pulling as hard as she could. He almost fell but twisted away, stumbling. One heavy boot connected with her head, hard, and Alex saw stars bursting in front of her eyes. She crawled as fast as she could, the gravel digging into her knees, but he made it to the gun before her. He picked it up and Alex reached futilely for the gun as she rolled, writhing for the pain that would mean death. It never came. Instead she felt the ground shake with concussion. She risked a look behind her and saw DuPre laying on the hardpack, a crimson puddle spreading beneath him and soaking into the ground. Alex craned her neck farther and Hank was there, re-holstering his weapon as he slid to her side. "Thank you," Alex said, and the world went black.

Chapter Twenty-Five

THE machine beeped. Again. For a place where people were constantly encouraging Alex to sleep, the interruptions never stopped. Alex opened one eye. The other, swollen from the bridge of her nose to her hairline and dissected by a row of ten stitches, stayed stubbornly shut. Her cast lay heavily on the stack of pillows. The room was dark, but Pasha's eyes glittered in the light from the hall. "Hey," Alex croaked.

He reached out and took her hand. "Hello, love," he replied. He leaned over, and Alex saw the dark circles under his eyes.

"You look like hell," she mumbled. "When did you last sleep?"

"Sometime in the 1700s," he replied, brushing her hair back from her forehead, careful to avoid her wound. "I am a bit hungry, though."

"Water, water, everywhere," Alex replied. Pasha smiled, still stroking her head. "I'm sorry," Alex said at last.

"There's nothing to be sorry for," he replied, "you did it." Alex felt sleep dragging her under.

"Love you," she said.

"Love you, too," Pasha replied, and then she was under again.

Alex slept on and off for the rest of the day. It seemed like she would never feel rested again. Still, thanks to some rest and amazing pain medications, by early evening Alex was feeling close to human again. Human enough that when Hank walked into her room she was able to smile.

"Tell me everything," he said.

"You first," she countered.

He chuckled and shook his head. "Neil was arraigned this morning. Lynx and Nathaniel this afternoon. They're all in jail, without bond. Neil tried very hard to be released on his own recognizance, but luckily the judge found him a flight risk. Nathaniel too."

"Lynx?" Alex said, a shiver that had nothing to do with the cold IV, running over her.

"Also no bond. I don't see Judge Abby shaken often, but I think even she was horrified. I thought about suggesting that they all be put in the same cell but decided against it."

"They'd certainly have something to talk about," Alex replied.

"We don't know anything yet, Nathaniel's lawyer is already pushing for a plea, but the DA said that she's confident that they'll be going to jail for a long, long time... Your turn."

Alex shrugged. "Fracture in my ankle; I'll be in a cast for the next couple of months. I have some stitches on my hand and my head," she waved her vaguely oven-mitt looking left hand in the air. "At least it's my stupid hand. Oh, a concussion. I'll be going home tomorrow. Or... somewhere anyway. I don't know that I want to go back there."

"I know a hotel..." Hank said.

"Don't you dare," Alex laughed, "I'll kick your ass too." He held up his hands in mock surrender. "Vinnie checked himself out before I woke up," she said, "but he did send these, via Dave."Alex gestured to a small bouquet of brightly colored suckers, each shaped like a male organ.

Hank glanced at them, and did a double-take. "Are those...?" Alex laughed.

"Yeah, yeah they are. Only Vinnie."

Hank shook his head. "Selah?" he asked.

"Already saw her. I made them wheel me down to her room before they stitched me up." She lowered her voice conspiratorially. "The intern loved me."

Hank chuckled in chagrin. "I bet they did. How's she doing?" Alex grew somber, started to pick at her nail before she remembered the mass of gauze.

"She's got a long road ahead of her, but she's going to be fine."

"It wasn't your fault, you know," Hank reassured. Alex looked away and said nothing.

Hank settled himself into the chair and tenderly took her hand. "This might not be the best time," he said, "but I was wondering if you'd be willing to let me take you out for a welcome home dinner?"

"New case?" she asked, her breath suddenly short. Hank shook his head. "Orders for protection?" another negative. He looked at her for a long moment and then leaned slowly in. The kiss started slowly then blossomed into hunger, wanting.

"You have no idea how long I've wanted to do that," he whispered when at last they broke apart.

"Maybe someday I'll find out," Alex said. His brow furrowed, then he burst out into laughter.

"Maybe you will," he said, "Maybe someday you will."

Also By Line By Lion

GHOST EYES

BOOK ONE OF THE ETERNITY SERIES

FOR TWO HUNDRED YEARS,
SHE HAS EXISTED HALF-DEAD.
ONLY ONE MAN HAS THE CHANCE
TO BRING HER BACK TO LIFE.

S. J. GARRETT

Vampocalypse

a novel by

E.S. Brown

Made in the USA
Columbia, SC
10 May 2024

35111243R00095